TRINITY WORKS ALONE

Trevor Holliday

Barnstork Press

Copyright © 2019 Trevor Holliday

All rights reserved

The characters and events portrayed in this book are fictitious. Any similarity to real persons, living or dead, is coincidental and not intended by the author.

No part of this book may be reproduced, or stored in a retrieval system, or transmitted in any form or by any means, electronic, mechanical, photocopying, recording, or otherwise, without express written permission of the publisher.

ISBN-13: 9798475894866
ISBN-10: 1477123456

Cover design by: John Holliday
Library of Congress Control Number: 2018675309
Printed in the United States of America

For Carolyn

CONTENTS

Title Page
Copyright
Dedication
The Drop Shot   1
Edison's Dream   7
A Persistent Cicada   16
Gedney   32
A Copy of Town and Country   34
Down at the Sunset Motel   42
At the Presidio Market   44
A Cardboard Clock   47
Amber Beads and a Concho Belt   50
The Long Expanse of Nothing   53
An Orchestra of Mauve   56
The Spires of Monument Valley   66
Rear-View Mirror   68
A Blood-Red Concrete Floor   71

The Puzzle's Blue Sky	77
The Quanah Parker Thing	81
Eyes a Paler Shade of Blue	84
Momento Mori	87
Not a Cop	91
No Drink in His Hand	97
Outside the Kashmir Tea Room	100
A-1 Extermination Company	107
Waiting for Gavino	113
The Watchmaker	118
John Wayne	122
Snake Venom	124
Barlow Knife	128
Exposure	130
Crown Victoria	132
Tribal Business	135
Anti-Psychotics	139
Lone Ranger meets the Fatal Bellman	142
Call Me Frank	145
Avoiding the Toxic Environment	147
A Call From the Emergency Room	151
Eyes of a Dragon	152
Presidio After Hours	162
Shower and Coffee	165

Red's House	166
Third-Page Story	169
Credentials in Order	170
Flashlight on the Staircase	173
Safe as Milk	175
Another Dead-End Blonde	177
On the QT	180
The Truth About Oracle	186
Some Weapon	191
The Pony	192
Seat Belts	194
Cracked Concrete	199
Two More Messages	201
Belly Dancing	202
A Minor League Curveball	206
Water Lilies	208
Roll of Nickels	212
Real Life Anthropology	216
The Missing Link	218
Raw Material	219
Motel Mescalito	222
Sober	228
Goodbye, My Brother	229
Prospecting	233

About The Author	235
Books By This Author	237

THE DROP SHOT

Frank Trinity played on the far side of the net on a side court at the Western Way.

The wooden tennis racket?

Part of the shtick.

Trinity might have been decades younger than his opponent. When the guy took off his cap Trinity noticed a thinning hairline and a sunburned scalp.

Trinity kept his own hair short, wore the darkest pair of Ray-Bans he could find, and still wore tennis whites.

It could have been the whites which threw the guy off. Nobody wore whites anymore, did they? Not in Tucson they didn't. Not even at the old Western Way Resort.

Now it was all cut-off denim shorts and headbands.

Not what Trinity grew up with.

The place was posh but understated, and Trinity felt at home there.

Then there was the matter of the wooden Davis tennis racket. Like the tennis whites, the racket was from a different era.

Trinity's era.

Trinity's opponent would never see sixty again, but still dressed and wanted to play like an eighteen-year-old. That was fine with Trinity, who intentionally whiffed a couple of the guy's serves.

Intentionally, but not obviously.

Trinity glanced at his Seiko 5 automatic watch. This game was child's play and it still wasn't eight in the morning.

Tucson in June meant early morning tennis or none at all.

The weather was a world away from the damp and chilly morning games he'd played while stationed at SHAPE headquarters in Belgium. As a young CID warrant officer, Trinity's main duty had been as a sort of guardian angel. He was often detailed with following the commanding officer's daughter, always from a discreet distance, and keeping her out of harm's way.

That was the year Trinity really learned to play tennis.

And learned how to make a little money along the way.

"You should upgrade that racket," the man said, holding up his own racket like exhibit A.

"I've thought about it," Trinity said. That much was true. He'd been thinking about it for years.

"... get more speed," the man said.

Was he out of breath so soon?

They always commented on the wooden racket.

Trinity had been using it since the sixties.

Trinity looked at it as if seeing it for the first time.

As if the racket had anything to do with it.

Just part of the shtick.

"How about a quick game for a hundred?" Trinity asked.

Casually. Conversationally. A just-between-the-two-of-us-guys kind of question.

No harm in asking. If the guy said no, Trinity would get some exercise. Instead, he got a how-can-this-shit-be-so-easy grin in return. The ploy almost always worked.

Trinity varied slams and drop shots just to make things interesting.

Peeling off five twenties from a money clip, Mr. Get-More-Speed didn't even know he'd been taken. He even insisted, in a halting, breathless voice, on exchanging cards. Trinity took the man's card and gave the man one of his own.

Trinity's cards were new:

Frank Trinity Investigations
98 Franklin Street
Tucson, Arizona

The man looked like he wanted to say something to Trinity, but quickly put the card into the clip and walked away when Tina approached.

Tina paused briefly court side.

A vision in her Western Way regulation shorts

and tennis shirt.

"That was nice of you, Frank."

She handed him a small green bottle of sparkling water.

Trinity patted a towel against the side of his face, held the bottle against his forehead, pulled off one of the twenties and gave it to Tina.

"Nice?"

"Yeah, that was sweet."

Tina was a nice kid, Trinity thought. Too young by a couple of years.

"You could have taken him for a whole lot more, right?"

Trinity smiled at Tina. In the bright sunshine of the Tucson morning, Tina was all questioning innocence. Too young by more than a couple of years.

"Sure, Tina."

The man was still on the opposite side of the court, stuffing his over-sized beast of a racket into a case.

Tina was right, of course. Trinity could have taken the guy for much, much more.

❈ ❈ ❈

Trinity's white Bronco didn't turn heads, but it accelerated like a refugee from hell. The truck meant business. Trinity nosed it out of the Western Way parking lot and shot into the morning foothills traffic.

Down Campbell, past St. Phillips, and out of the desert.

Heat radiated from the asphalt. People were heading to their jobs in the city. At the light on the corner of Campbell and Glenn, a knockout blonde in a bright yellow Mercedes smiled at Trinity.

Things were good for Trinity. Even on a day promising heat over 110 degrees, he could stay cool.

Heading south.

Cannonball Adderley blasting from the speakers.

Mercy,

Mercy,

Mercy...

The interior of the Bronco was an icy cocoon. What more did he need?

Nada.

He thought about Tina. She was just about the same age as Angela, the commanding officer's daughter. Trinity kept Angela safe that year. It hadn't been easy. Angela had been a wildcat. It had been memorable, but it seemed like a hundred years ago.

That had been the year before Trinity met Valerie Girard. Meeting Valerie and falling in love changed everything in Trinity's world. He proposed to her in French; she helped him improve his schoolboy French. They were going to be married in her hometown of Lyon. And then Valerie died. Killed by an out-of-control driver on a dark rainy night in Lyon's ancient quarter. Trinity's life went dark.

He thought about Tina.

The last thing he needed was a twenty-something girl in his life. Even for an afternoon.

After a shower, he would relax for a while underneath the vigas on the patio behind his Presidio adobe.

The four twenty dollar bills were spread on the leather passenger seat where he'd tossed them.

Eighty bucks.

One short of the Jackson Five.

He didn't need the money. Trinity was strictly a recreational player.

What did he need?

Trinity didn't need a thing. He just needed to stay cool. He would use the twenties for breakfast money.

He would have breakfast at the Presidio Market. Lesley and April, the women who ran the place, served good breakfasts and great coffee. It was Trinity's regular spot.

So what did he need?

He didn't need a new racket.

He looked over at his wooden Davis.

This one worked just fine.

EDISON'S DREAM

The crow awakened him from some kind of vivid dream, but by the time he opened his eyes Edison Graves could barely remember what the dream was about.

Was the crow in the dream, or was it flying high above Edison's old Ford F-150?

The sun-bleached red truck was older than Edison.

He had had some beers the night before, maybe more than a few, but he had only the slightest trace of a hangover.

That was nice.

He pushed the gray Pendleton blanket aside and looked out over the broad orange panorama of the high desert morning. He was north of Holbrook, Arizona. Just barely on the Navajo Nation.

The clock on his truck's dashboard showed it was almost eight.

Time to make some coffee. Almost eight and

the cornflower blue sky was already shimmering in the heat of the day. Edison slammed the truck door shut with a satisfying clang, dropped the tailgate and set up the green camp stove. While the propane hissed, Edison pulled out the eight cup percolator and scooped enough for two strong cups of java. The smell of the coffee permeated the air while Edison sat on the tailgate, closed his eyes and meditated about the coming day.

The crow had awakened him, and Edison felt he should remember the dream. Something about it seemed significant but just out of reach.

Coffee would be ready.

Probably just as well the bird awakened him.

When he got back in the truck he would need to backtrack. He hoped he had enough gas in the tank. The register was unreliable. Edison clanked the side of the jerry can strapped inside the bed of the truck.

Empty.

He'd have to hope for the best.

Backtrack. Three miles back to Holbrook? Fifteen? Twenty? He looked at the horizon. There wasn't a sign nearby, just the mountains in the distance. Too hard to tell how far from town he was.

He'd backtrack to Holbrook to see Tasha and then he would pick up Livingston.

It wouldn't be a problem. It was still early. His first bull ride wasn't for hours.

Edison was glad he had apparently abandoned

the festivities last night and slept in the desert. The last thing he wanted to hear was the bullshit from the other riders. Especially not from Duane.

College-boy... White-boy... Bad enough from the other riders, but from his own younger brother Duane, it was intolerable.

At least, Edison thought, Livingston never started that shit.

What they really were asking him was the same question Edison asked himself whenever he went to Holbrook.

He'd asked himself the same question last night.

What was he doing here?

He picked up the piece of cottonwood he'd been working on. One of these days it would be a flute. Right now it wasn't cooperating.

He patted the wood against his hand. You could smash in a skull with this thing.

Wasn't there a better way of testing himself than to drive five hours north of Tucson to get on the back of a fifteen hundred pound bull? Why not leave it to those other guys with their flashy red pickups and prize belt buckles?

Leave it to the guys who'd never left the reservation, and never would. Guys who's idea of a big time was a truck ride to Holbrook for a suitcase of beer.

Leave that to Duane. Duane was joining their ranks.

He hoped he could convince Livingston to

move. It was time for his older brother to leave the old motel and go home.

Edison worked himself out of the cab. His knee hurt like hell today. The crow flew off with a loud whoosh-whoosh.

What was it about crows?

Edison could hear Adelle's voice. They're the fatal bellman... something like that. It had been a long time. Edison scratched his knee. Maybe it wasn't even crows.

Maybe it was owls.

He pulled his striped Wrangler shirt on, pushed the tail into the front of his jeans, and looked across the top of the mesa at the mountain in the distance. Peabody Coal had ground the top of the the thing down like a worn pencil.

Edison poured the coffee into his thermos. If he needed more later he could get some in town. Then go see Tasha, pick up Livingston, and get to the rodeo grounds in time to ride.

Edison had never lived in Holbrook.

He had grown up north of Holbrook, way up near the Utah line.

He had left Monument Valley High School years ago on a white man's scholarship to Dartmouth.

Being Ivy League, Dartmouth didn't give football scholarships, but somehow there had been money for a Navajo with decent test scores who played cornerback like the ghost of Jim Thorpe.

He had fallen in love.

He thought it was with Adelle Anderson who had been assigned as his tutor. She was a couple of years older than him and from New Jersey. But he hadn't fallen in love with Adelle. He'd fallen for Shakespeare. Adelle wanted to hear the mythology of Edison's people. Edison wanted to hear Adelle give voice to Ophelia. He'd blown out his knee during his junior year. He remembered the popping sound that came before the searing pain. People had said that he could have gone pro. Adelle cried when she saw him in the post-op bed at Dartmouth-Hitchcock.

Then she started going out with a pre-law guy. A white guy, of course. Edison still remembered Adelle's face when Edison confronted the two of them. Still could remember the shock he felt confronting his own violence.

Edison had limped away that night with the man crumpled in the street and Adelle crying.

He never saw her again.

He now lived in Tucson, working on a masters in literature that might take forever if he was lucky. He was dating another woman now, another graduate student. She had gone to Holbrook with him months ago. Anything relating to Native culture turned her on.

She'd met Tasha, Livingston and Duane.

She hung on every single word of Livingston's ravings.

She had wanted to go with Edison on this trip

too. He'd seen the disappointment in her eyes when he told her he wouldn't take her.

Maybe he wasn't ready for another disappointment, or maybe he was simply setting himself up for more heartache.

Why else had he shared so much with this woman, who really wasn't all that different from Adelle?

Livingston and Tasha, his brother and sister-in-law, had practically raised Edison and Duane. They left the reservation with Duane while Edison was in New Hampshire.

Livingston and Tasha had moved to Holbrook. They thought Duane would do better there.

Better than what? Edison wondered. He shook his head. The move to Holbrook didn't make a whole lot of sense.

❉ ❉ ❉

Despite bordering I-10 and the Navajo Reservation, Holbrook was a white man's town. Three years later, Tasha was still waiting tables at the Giant Truck Stop and Duane had all but become a gang-banger. Livingston had semi-officially moved out of the little house on Florida Street and was doing a whole lot of nothing.

Livingston still competed in Indian rodeos every so often, hoping State Compensation didn't catch on.

In between the rodeos, he drank whiskey.

Lately, of course, it had been the peyote.

Livingston claimed to have experienced an epiphany in the desert near the Petrified Forest. He'd spent a lot of time talking about it during Edison's last visit.

Of course Edison's girlfriend had been enthralled. As if Livingston were something other than what Edison knew he was, a broken-down bull rider with broken down dreams.

So of course she wanted to go to Holbrook. Why hadn't he just brought her?

Edison drove through McDonalds and ordered two sausage biscuits. The entry and fee for the All-Indian Rodeo was rolled up next to him on the seat. Edison flattened it out. A few trivial prizes would be awarded at the rodeo but Edison didn't care about them. He was here for Livingston's sake. If Livingston wanted Edison to compete, Edison would be there. His knee felt worse than ever and so did his head.

He poured some coffee from his thermos. Rubbed his leg. He would be ready.

At the truck stop, Tasha hugged him and looked like she was going to cry. "Didn't you bring your girlfriend?" she said.

Edison shook his head.

Tasha called over to the other waitress, "Debbie, come see my handsome little brother."

Debbie looked impressed. "You're the other bull rider?"

He smiled. "That's me."

"You must be crazy."

Edison shook his head no. He wasn't the crazy one in the family. Livingston? Yes. Duane? No question. Duane was crazy. But not him. Not Edison. Edison always kept himself straight.

Tasha was beaming. "He's practically a professor."

Except that one time. The one time outside the bar in Hanover. He remembered the sound his fist made, pounding the guy's face. And he remembered the sound of Adelle's scream.

Tasha fluttered around him. "You want something? Pie? Coffee?"

Edison shook his head. "Got it in the truck. I figured I'd check in on Livingston."

Tasha's expression fell. Debbie walked back toward the kitchen. "He's still at that place," she said. Edison knew she was talking about the Sunset Motel. Livingston had lived there off and on since Tasha had thrown him out. "But he won't be there now. He goes down to the tracks every day."

Edison hugged her.

"Take it easy," he said.

Tasha's eyes flashed.

"He needs you, Little Brother. You shouldn't have left."

Tasha was right, Edison thought, getting back in the pickup. Who the hell did he think he was? He shouldn't have left.

And maybe more importantly, he shouldn't have come back.

"I'll find him," he said.

"You be careful."

Debbie, the other waitress returned from the kitchen.

"Win one of those buckles, Edison."

"If I do," he said, "I'll bring it back here."

A PERSISTENT CICADA

Trinity parked the Bronco in front of his house on Franklin Street, stooped to pick up the paper before unlocking his front door.

Running laps in hell might be cooler than playing tennis in this heat. This time of day sweat turned to salt on the skin. Inevitably, Trinity thought, somebody would bring up the virtues of dry heat.

Dry like a blast oven. I should have a swimming pool, he thought. At this point, a plastic wading pool would be fine. Instead, he had hard caliche and a couple of mesquites. In one of the trees, a persistent cicada made high-pitched droning noises.

Love-sick mating calls. Not a bad sound if you were a cicada.

Trinity wished it would drown out the sounds of his neighbor's argument.

"I don't care what you say, you son-of-a-bitch," Karma Blue yelled at her partner Leonard.

Karma Blue outweighed Leonard by a good fifty pounds and yelled at him daily. From behind the oleanders separating their houses, Trinity saw Leonard sitting on an aluminum folding chair in front of a small barbecue. Eight o'clock meant that Leonard would be stoned.

The subject, a familiar one for Karma Blue, was Leonard's ongoing, unrepentant infidelity.

"Just keep screwing her, you bastard. Just keep screwing her..." Karma Blue's voice was like a dental drill. "I'll put a knife in your lying heart and twist it off."

It wasn't the summer of love for these two.

Trinity felt sorry for Leonard, who was a pretty nice guy when Karma Blue wasn't around. And Karma Blue herself didn't exactly mirror the image portrayed on fliers she put up advertising her services as a 'compassionate healing medium.'

Leonard wasn't responding to Karma Blue. He gave a weak wave when he saw Trinity looking at him. A kind of I'm-deep-into-my-zen-master-meditation wave.

Meaning Leonard was stoned as hell.

❋ ❋ ❋

Trinity's answering machine was flashing. The adobe walls, almost three feet of hardened mud, kept out light and heat. The low thrum of the swamp cooler reassured Trinity that his house would stay cool today.

Inside, the house smelled earthy. It was the smell of the old west, Trinity imagined.

The cooler's moist straw pads, the ocotillo ribs of the high ceiling, a slight breeze from an old metal fan made it Trinity's home. Dark and cool.

He loved it.

It had been a smart move, buying the place.

Later, Trinity found out Georges Simenon had lived on Franklin back in the fifties.

Inspector Maigret in Tucson.

As a warrant officer, Trinity had made decent money. With little to spend it on during his last few years overseas, he'd banked most of his pay.

Since Valerie.

Before Valerie, he'd thrown his money away.

The answering machine flashed on and off. It was persistent.

Needing light, Trinity found the switch beneath the tin sconce. A diffused glow bathed the light ochre walls of the front room. He propped the Davis racket against the smooth cobblestone pillar of his bookshelf. The book he bought yesterday at Value Village still lay open, flapping gently in the churned air of the swamp cooler.

RARE EARTH: PROSPECTING IN ARIZONA and NORTHERN SONORA - 1924 Edition.

If nothing else, the maps and illustrations were worth more than the buck he had paid for the dusty volume.

Trinity grabbed a towel from the stack next to the bathroom. He glanced at the answering machine then flipped the fan speed up on the cooler. The pages in the heavy book flipped. Dust and water spewed from the cooler. Trinity grabbed the book and wedged it horizontally on the already packed bookcase.

In the kitchen, he took a bottle of San Pellegrino, poured a glass and glanced at the front page of the newspaper. A full color shot of a man stirring a kettle over a fire accompanied an article about the Solar People gearing up for their annual mid-summer roll in the mud later in the week. Some place up near Oracle. The skinny guy claimed he had given up six-figures annually to cook lunches for the migratory tribe.

Sure thing, Trinity thought.

Trinity got up, tossed aside the paper, threw the towel into the sink and soaked it. The water was lukewarm. Like most water in Tucson this time of year, the ground and pipes heated it. Trinity put ice cubes into the towel and wrapped it around his head.

The icy towel felt good against his forehead.

The first message was from a guy selling solar water heaters.

Fat chance, Trinity thought. I'll just use Karma Blue and Leonard's method. His neighbors ran water for showers through a black hose they'd draped onto their roof.

The cicada in the mesquite continued its rattling whine joined by a siren heading south past the Tucson Electric Company.

The second message grabbed Trinity's attention.

The man sounded like he was gasping for air.

"Frank Trinity?" the man on the tape paused, as if waiting for Trinity to respond.

The cicada stopped buzzing. Trinity took a swig of the San Pellegrino.

He recognized the voice.

"My name is Brooks... Edward D. Brooks."

"Shit," Trinity said. "Shit, shit, shit."

Talking back to the answering machine was a hold-over army habit, like eating quickly and waiting in line. He pulled the wrinkled card from his wallet.

Sure enough. The tennis player from the Western Way.

Edward D. Brooks.

❉ ❉ ❉

"Anyway," Brooks said. "I've got a little problem with my daughter. I didn't want to talk with you about it in public. But I thought maybe you could help. I'm at the end of my rope. That's why I'm calling you."

Trinity looked over at the swamp cooler which was starting to make a funny sound. Would he need to replace it?

"I'm listening," he said to the machine.

Public? Since when was an empty tennis court public?

The guy must not have wanted to talk around Tina. As if Tina was listening.

Trinity tossed the towel onto the floor. "Hurry up."

"My daughter is..."

Edward D. Brooks hesitated. Just like he had at the Western Way.

Still gasping. "Could we set up an appointment? Is that how you work?"

Brooks rattled off the same address and phone number printed on his card.

"I really don't want to involve the police," Brooks said. "I don't see how they could help."

The answering machine beeped.

Trinity grabbed a pad and listened to the message again. Something about the last part...

He hit the play button a third time.

"I don't see how they could help."

Edward D. Brooks slurred the last words.

Trinity thought about the message as he stood in the shower. The daughter was... what?

Edward D. Brooks sounded drunk.

Maybe he was half in the bag during the game. Trinity shook his head. So, he'd taken a hundred bucks from a drunk.

Classy.

Trinity shrugged. At least they'd both gotten some exercise.

Trinity thought about the message while putting on a fresh pair of blue jeans and a starched white shirt.

He needed to talk to the laundry about the starch. He liked his shirts to stand up on their own.

Edward D. Brooks.

Before today, that name meant nothing to Trinity.

Zip point shit.

Edward D. Brooks.

Trinity pulled on his Tony Lamas and looked under the clutter of the kitchen table for a street map. Brooks lived somewhere up in the foothills.

Camino del Vaca.

Three part Spanish street names generally meant money, and something about the message sounded like trouble. He slipped his snub nose into a shoulder holster and wrapped both of them with a blue summerweight blazer.

Summer-weight for somewhere other than Tucson.

The sun nearly knocked him over as he kicked his front door shut.

✻ ✻ ✻

Brooks lived in an old Santa Fe style house. The kind that stays low to the ground like a dust devil and sprawls behind the cover of desert vegetation.

Standing at the front door, Trinity looked at the long expanse of the Tucson skyline, trying to pick his neighborhood out of the brownish haze spreading from A Mountain to the university.

Nothing ostentatious about the house. Its understatement practically screamed money.

Brooks answered the door himself, holding what Trinity guessed wasn't his first gin and tonic of the day. He looked like a man not sure if his wife was returning and not sure exactly whether he should celebrate or mourn.

"Trinity," Brooks said, squinting into unaccustomed midday sunlight, "you came quickly. I thought you'd call before you headed up."

"You said you needed help. I figured you didn't mean tomorrow."

"It's a scorcher out today. Come on in." Brooks looked apologetic. "Good thing we got our game in early."

"Yeah," Trinity said, "it's just me and the mad dogs out today."

The two men stood in a front door framing a dark interior.

"I'm in your debt, Mr. Trinity." A small patch of peeling red skin poked from the top of Brook's balding scalp. It looked even worse than it had during the game.

Brooks scratched the patch while leading Trinity into the living room. Beams from a bank of track lights bathed two enormous abstract oil paintings. The paintings were not the work of an amateur. Someone had used up a lot of paint and canvas on them. Someone who knew what they were doing.

"Can I offer you something?" Brooks held up his nearly empty tumbler like a first-place trophy in a tippling tournament. "I'm drinking gin."

"I'm drinking water." Trinity said.

Brooks' choice of gin wasn't surprising. The slur in his voice spoke of morning drinking.

Gin, Trinity thought, a solid choice for pre-lunch inebriation.

"On the phone you mentioned your daughter?"

Brooks walked to a side table and picked up a green pitcher shaped like a fish. It gurgled as he poured. His hand trembled slightly handing the water to Trinity.

"I didn't want to talk in front of that girl." Brooks raised his eyebrows then interrupted himself. "I'm sorry the place is such a mess." He waved his arm as if to include the entire house. "As you can see, I'm not much of a housekeeper."

Brooks perched on the couch closest to Trinity. He took another sip of the gin. Smiled. "Maid's day off, too. That's the worst thing."

Despite what Brooks had said, the room was as neat as viewing day at the funeral home.

Trinity drank the tepid water.

If that's the worst thing in his life, Trinity thought, this guy's got it made.

He nodded. If Brooks wanted to talk about housekeeping, Trinity would give it a minute or two.

"Mr. Trinity, I want you to know that my daughter is absolutely the most precious thing to me in my life. Absolutely the most precious. And I'm a terrible father."

Brooks paused and brought the back of his hand toward his eye.

"The most precious daughter a man could have, and all I do is drink gin in the morning and call someone I don't even know for help."

Trinity guessed he was that someone.

"Well, I do know you," Brooks said, "in a manner of speaking."

"It's almost afternoon, Brooks. Is your daughter in trouble?"

"That's just it. If I knew that, I wouldn't have called you, would I?"

Brooks turned his face toward Trinity.

"The truth is that I can't find out. Nobody seems to know where she is."

"What makes you think your daughter is in trouble?"

"Wouldn't you think so?"

Brooks stared at Trinity.

"I mean, wouldn't you think so?"

He put the drink down on the arm of the leather couch and a ring of sweat spread out from the glass.

Trinity shrugged.

"I'm sorry, Trinity. I haven't really told you anything, have I?"

"Not really. You said you were a lousy father. So what?"

"I'm very sorry." Brooks struggled to regain his composure. His hand reached toward his sunburned patch of scalp. He pushed a thin lock of hair back into place covering the patch and the balding spot surrounding it.

Things were out of order in Edward Brooks' life, Trinity thought, and it wasn't just his hair.

"Why don't you try telling me what's going on."

"Lisa is a good girl. Oh, she has her moments, don't get me wrong. But she really is the sweetest thing."

An artificial smile crossed his face. It was a welcome relief from self-pity.

"The sweetest thing in the world."

It was established, Trinity thought. Lisa Brooks was both the sweetest thing in the world and the most precious thing in her father's life.

He was beginning to feel sympathy for the girl.

"How long has your daughter been missing?"

Brooks slumped down on the couch. "I haven't seen her since the start of summer semester," he said, "even before that, really. She lives in a sorority house, which is fine with me." Brooks waved his down-turned palms away from himself like an umpire signaling a runner safe.

Trinity watched Brooks. The man looked as if he was deciding whether or not to continue. Or like a man deciding if he should tell the truth or lie.

Brooks picked up his drink from the couch and

toyed with it.

"She always checks in. Oh, I know what you're probably thinking, but she doesn't just come up here for her allowance. She does her laundry here, brings her friends up to swim. It's nice having kids around. She has a nice set of friends. I couldn't be happier with them."

Brooks looked at Trinity for approval. The lock of hair dropped back down and with a practiced motion Brooks slapped it back precisely, like a candidate for the comb-over hall of fame.

"You haven't heard from her in how long?"

"She's called. Three times actually, asking for money. Once for summer tuition, room and board. Twice more to top up her allowance."

He shrugged as if to ask what he could do.

"Naturally I put the money in her account."

"Naturally," Trinity repeated. "How much money each time?"

The question made Brooks visibly uncomfortable. Not enough to squirm, but enough to make him reach for his hair.

"Enough to cover it. Plenty I suppose. You probably would think I indulge her."

Trinity shrugged. "She's your daughter."

"Her mother thinks that I've spoiled her. But better that than neglect, wouldn't you say? Anyway, that's not the problem."

It wasn't the problem that made him call me, Trinity thought.

"Did you ask her where she was calling from?"

Brooks stared at Trinity.

"What do you suppose was the first thing I asked her? She wouldn't tell me anything. That's unusual for us. We've got a better relationship than that."

Edward Brooks could change his tone from self-pity to sarcasm to pious self-satisfaction in seconds.

Trinity thought about the hundred dollars he'd taken from Brooks on the tennis court earlier.

He didn't regret it a bit.

Brooks had looked startled when asked about the money he'd given to his daughter. The amount wasn't the question, he had wanted to show Trinity how tasteless he found the entire topic.

"She's not at the sorority house?" Trinity tried guiding the conversation back to the girl.

"None of the girls have seen her."

"When was her last phone call?"

"Before I called you, as a matter of fact."

"She asked for money?"

"Of course."

"Did she sound different?"

"No. Only in the way that I've already said. She was evasive. For Lisa that's unusual."

"Did she register for classes?"

"I imagine she must have, but I can't get anywhere with the school. They said something about a privacy act before they hung up. But she's my daughter… Shouldn't I be able to find out if she's enrolled in classes? I mean, shouldn't I?"

Brooks' words trailed off in a decrescendo.

"I've got pictures of Lisa," he said, "won't you need one?"

He took a photo from the table next to the couch, pulled it from a silver frame and handed it to Trinity.

The ten by eight inch black and white showed a girl seated sideways to the camera, her hands in her lap.

"She was in high school when this was taken," Brooks said. "It's a good likeness, I think."

There was nothing to find out from Lisa's expression. She was a pretty blonde girl. A nice smile for the camera. There was no way to see what she looked like now.

"Nothing more recent?"

Brooks shook his head and made a dismissive gesture with his hand.

"I just hope I'm not over-reacting," he said. "It could turn out to be nothing. But I called you just in case. I meant to call someone. I just didn't know who. I can pay your regular fee, whatever that is."

"You haven't called the police?"

Brooks stared at Trinity.

"If it turns out to be nothing, I don't want to involve the authorities."

"I hope it's nothing," Trinity said. "But if you thought that, you wouldn't have called me. I charge by the day, plus expenses."

"Expenses?" Brooks gave Trinity what might have passed for a hard look.

"Bribes and mileage."

Brooks pulled out a checkbook without flinching.

"Lisa's mother is still living?" Trinity took the check and glanced at it before folding it into his shirt pocket. He liked the amount Brooks had written on the check. If Brooks still thought he was in Trinity's debt, the check would help.

"Her Royal Highness? Alive and well and living with her dentist husband in El Encanto. She blames everything on me, naturally. I wish you could have heard her on the phone this morning."

Trinity stood up and turned toward the front door.

"I'll need her address and phone number. While you're at it you can write down the names of Lisa's friends."

Brooks nodded.

"I'll get Arlene's address."

He got up from his perch on the couch.

"It may take awhile. Make yourself comfortable."

He pointed at Trinity's water and laughed.

"Have some booze, for crying out loud. That stuff will kill you."

With Brooks out of the room, Trinity took a closer look at the paintings. They were good. Two-fisted abstracts with an edge he liked.

Brooks came back into the room holding an address book.

"I don't have the slightest idea how to get in

touch with her friends. I know them by sight, but in the summer I'm sure they part with the four winds. Maybe check with the sorority."

On his way out the door, Trinity noticed a small picture on the hallway table of Brooks carrying a small girl on his shoulders. The girl couldn't have been more than five. The shot had been taken at Sabino Canyon's Seven Falls. Brooks and the girl were both smiling madly for the camera.

Trinity pointed at the photograph. "Lisa?"

Brooks nodded.

"Another lifetime," he said. "Years and years ago."

GEDNEY

Edison may not have known Holbrook well, but he knew how to get to the railroad tracks.

The railroad bisected the town and the truck stop was about two miles away.

He pulled past the petrified wood shop, the one with the concrete dinosaurs in front, and turned the truck left before the train tracks. There was no train coming now but Edison had seen traffic backed up all the way to the old courthouse when one of the Santa Fe trains lumbered through.

Livingston's friend Gedney sat on the curb outside the pawnshop. He looked at Edison when he came up to him. The place was still closed, but the barred windows revealed rows of bottles inside.

Gedney raised his hand in a salute. His face was a pitted red complexion with a shock of uncut black hair falling down to a red nose.

"You seen Livingston?" Edison asked.

"Not for a little while," Gedney said. "Should be here pretty soon though."

He ran his hand along the dusty concrete

sidewalk, inviting Edison to sit.

"Pretty soon, unless he's gone fishing."

Gedney laughed.

Edison nodded. A pretty good joke. Where would you go fishing in Holbrook? Hilarious.

"I'll be seeing you then," Edison said, turning back toward his truck.

"Okay then," Gedney said. "Hey…"

Edison turned back.

Gedney shook his head and held out his hand, palm up. "Hey," he said, "how 'bout some money?"

Edison pulled out his wallet and took out three, then four one dollar bills.

Gedney nodded. Smoothed the bills on the top of the shiny knee of his pants.

"Livingston's your brother?"

Edison nodded.

Gedney knew that. He was bullshitting. He grimaced, showed a mouth full of darkened teeth, shook his head. "Your brother's been kind of messed up."

So, what else is new, Edison thought. Livingston had been a little more than messed up for a while.

"What do you mean?" Edison said.

"Crazy," Gedney said.

He held up his index finger and spun it around his ear.

"Hearing stuff. Hanging out with crazy people."

A COPY OF TOWN AND COUNTRY

Trinity parked the Bronco in the alley behind the row of sorority and fraternity houses clustered along the north side of the university. An automatic sprinkler kicked on and hissed over the well-manicured lawn, spraying Trinity's white shirt with a fine mist.

A serious looking girl wearing tortoiseshell glasses and a sleeveless dress opened the door for Trinity.

"I'm looking for Lisa Brooks. Do you know if she's here?"

The girl invited him into the foyer. Behind her, the living room was decorated in pastels and potted plants. The sound of a Thelonious Monk piece drifted in like a heavy perfume.

"I just came here for the summer," the girl said. "I take it she lives here during the year? If you want to wait, I'll get someone who would know."

Trinity sat on the corner of a piano bench. He thumbed through a copy of *Town and Country*.

"Oh by the way," the girl said from the door, "who should I say is asking?

"Frank."

"Okay, Frank. Wait right there."

"I'm not going anywhere."

The magazine was still current. Trinity glanced at an article about a debutante ball held in Grosse Pointe.

"You're looking for Lisa Brooks?" The voice of the sleek, well-tanned woman framed in the doorway was East Coast. Other than the fact that it was Tucson, the woman could have been in town for a regatta.

Trinity dropped the magazine onto the couch and stood up. The woman was attractive in a polished way that spoke of privilege and good exercise habits.

"Her father asked me to. I'm a friend of the family. My name is Frank Trinity."

"Pamela Chambers. I'm the house advisor." She thrust her hand out for Trinity. "I'm certainly glad to speak with you. What is going on with Lisa?"

Emphasis, though slight, on the word "on."

She slid onto the sofa, tucking a leg beneath herself.

"I hope you can tell me. Her parents are worried about her."

"You know I'm sorry, Mr. Trinity. I really am. I'm afraid though, that I won't be much help to you. I can't say I know Lisa well. Most of the girls here at the house think that I'm ancient, but I'm not even thirty yet." She smiled. "I understand that's just entering the prime of life."

Trinity nodded. "That's my experience."

Pamela laughed. "Then it must be true. Anyway, I really don't spend much time here. I duck in here when I can, but I don't live here. I have a job in addition to my classes to make ends meet."

"So you might not have seen her anyway?"

"That's right," Pamela said, "the fact is, I have a whole separate life apart from this place."

She looked a little like Valerie, Trinity thought.

For whatever reason, Trinity had been thinking about Valerie a lot today. She would have been what, thirty-eight? Thirty-nine. Wasn't that just entering the prime of life? He thought about the gentle way Valerie would correct his pronunciation and the ease with which she would order in their favorite restaurants. Maybe Tina, the girl at the Westward Way, had started him thinking of Valerie. Tina was nice, just like this woman at the sorority house was nice. It was a world full of nice women.

Pamela laughed. "You've made my day." She put her finger on her chin and light from the window fell on her arms. "So what can I tell you about Lisa?"

"When was the last time you saw her?"

Pamela shook her head. "Honestly, I don't even know if she finished the semester. I don't remember seeing her at any of the spring chapter meetings. But that's not unusual. Enthusiasm decreases around here towards the end of the year. And I've been so busy working on my thesis..."

Trinity was inspecting a composite on the wall. Lisa wore a long dress, very much like all the other girls smiling for the camera. It could have been the starting lineup for the Grosse Pointe Cotillion.

In far left field, Miss Lisa Brooks...

"My thesis is in anthropology, if you're interested."

"This is the most recent shot of Lisa?"

"Probably, but you're welcome to check the scrapbook." She stood up and picked up a leather-covered album from the end-table. Thelonious Monk finished "Round Midnight" and hammered the opening of "Bemsha Swing." Pamela peered at the book over Trinity's shoulder. She stood close behind him. Close enough for Trinity to smell her perfume and feel her hip against his back.

Promise her anything, he thought, but give her Arpege.

He closed his eyes briefly.

Dating himself.

"Here she is, I think." The picture was slightly out of focus, but Trinity recognized Lisa in cut-offs and a tee shirt with the Greek lettering of the sorority.

"May I take this?"

Pamela shifted away abruptly. "I don't see why not. I'm worried too. Her father doesn't know where she is?"

"I'm helping him find her. If you knew her roommate's name, that would be a big help. If she has a boyfriend. That kind of thing."

"No roommate, I'm afraid." Pamela frowned. "You should talk to Wendy Chandler. They're friends. Wendy lives in town somewhere. Sorry, I don't know her very well. I did my undergraduate work in Pennsylvania. I just came here for grad school. Hold on, I'll give you Wendy's address." Pamela walked back to the couch.

It occurred to Trinity that the heavy silver and turquoise of Pamela's squash blossom necklace might seem incongruous paired with her sleeveless white pullover. But it was difficult to imagine this house advisor wearing anything less than flattering.

"I don't think there's any boyfriend on the scene, but I couldn't say for sure."

"Anything else you can think of?"

"Well, Lisa spent a lot of time last winter at the Omega House."

"That's a frat?"

Pamela nodded. "At least until they get kicked off campus again. They have a terrible reputation. Probably the worst house of campus. Somebody set us up with them for a mixer last fall. What a total disaster." Her nose wrinkled at the repugnant memory of the worst house on campus.

"Lisa made friends there?"

Pamela turned her face, her fingertips touching

the turquoise center of the necklace.

"That's what I've heard. I haven't talked to anyone about it, but I'm sure Lisa wasn't the only girl involved. Though what any of our girls would see in the place I'll never know."

She hesitated.

"I probably don't want to know."

There were a few reasons Trinity could think of. Primordial urges darker than those typically experienced in upper division anthropology seminars.

Pamela Chambers might have experienced them. Possibly.

But mixer or no mixer, she was telling Trinity that she herself would never darken the door of a place like Omega.

"You like Thelonious Monk?" he asked.

Her face brightened. "He's fabulous. I can't believe you recognize him."

Trinity smiled. "Couldn't miss him. You could give me the blindfold test."

"Sounds fun," she laughed, "what else do you like?"

He pressed his fingers together. "Only Thelonious... And the Ramones."

Pamela nodded then smiled. She might be a jazz enthusiast, but she wasn't a snob. Trinity liked that.

"I'd like Wendy's address, if you can get it for me. I'll leave my card with you in case anything turns up you think I should know about."

It was the same card he'd given Lisa's father.

Pamela held it as if she had found it under a rock.

"I thought you were a friend of the family..."

"We're just getting acquainted," Trinity said, "can you get the address for me?"

"Wait right here. I'll get it for you." Her voice stiffened like an orchid left in the deep freeze.

"I'm not going anywhere," he said.

Pamela had left the room, leaving her scent lingering and the memory of her disapproving look.

He wasn't going anywhere. He sat waiting on the couch. He picked up the magazine again and looked at an advertisement for a hotel in Aruba.

You need a break, he thought, after a tough debutante season.

❈ ❈ ❈

It took Pamela a few minutes to find the address. Long enough for a shadow from the afternoon sun to fall across the pastel-colored room. Long enough for Thelonious Monk to leave his piano and be replaced by the silence of the darkened room.

Long enough for Trinity to wonder if he needed to start a new investigation.

Pamela returned with composure regained and lipstick reapplied.

"I finally found it." She stood up straight,

smiling a perfect Miss Porter's smile at Trinity. Obviously, Pamela knew the importance of good posture. "Sorry about my little contretemps," she said. "You just caught me off guard." She held out a piece of ivory colored stationary. "I put my telephone number on there, too." The precise lettering was written in the blue ink of a fountain pen. She looked at Trinity. "Let me know if there is anything I can do to help you."

She stood next to the door. The perfect hostess, showing her guests out at the end of a perfectly delightful evening, her fingers tracing the heavy silver of the necklace.

The sound of a Native American flute crept into the room.

Trinity listened. "You switch from bebop in the evening?"

She laughed. "Carlos Nakai. My latest obsession."

Trinity nodded. The flute was cool and subtle and spoke of canyons and mystery. He looked at Pamela's card. If he needed any help she would be right at the top of his list.

He tucked the card in his shirt pocket.

DOWN AT THE SUNSET MOTEL

Room seventeen at the Sunset Motel was a corner unit with an alley view. Edison knew the owner of the place let Livingston stay week to week and pay with his compensation checks and a few odd jobs around the place. Edison tried not to visit the motel. Seeing Livingston drunk on the street was less depressing for Edison than the sight of his brother lying on his bed in this fleabag.

He took his time driving to the motel. Needing more coffee, he stopped at the U-Totem near the place. After screwing plastic lids onto two cups of black coffee, Edison asked the clerk for a pint of Ten High.

The leathery-skinned clerk grinned at Edison. "A little hair of the dog, I guess?"

Edison didn't bother to explain. His brother needed it like any medicine. What did the guy care and what business was it of his anyway?

The motel was mostly abandoned. Some of the windows were boarded up with spray-painted plywood. Others, like Livingston's, had towels and sheets hung to keep out the sun's persistent shine.

Livingston had a Dallas Cowboy towel in the window. His home-sweet-home. It wasn't always like this. What changed in his brother's life? Had it been something Edison did? Maybe Tasha was right. If Edison hadn't taken the scholarship, he could have stayed on the rez and kept an eye on Livingston.

Why Dartmouth? He could have taken college classes near Kayenta or gone to Northern Arizona University in Flagstaff. He would have been fine.

Edison knocked on the flimsy hollow core of Livingston's door. There was no answer.

Livingston was probably dead to the world.

The door was open. Livingston never locked a door.

Edison looked around the wreck of a room. Smashed up everywhere. A broken mirror and lamp and all Livingston's clothes hanging out of his dresser.

Livingston lay in the center of the room on a dingy brown carpet, a dark puddle surrounding him from the stab wound in the chest.

AT THE PRESIDIO MARKET

April waved at Trinity as he took a table on the veranda of the Presidio Market.

"Here you go, Frank."

She brought a pitcher of water to his table and smiling, lightly touched his shoulder.

"God Almighty," she said. She pointing at the blue jacket he held under his arm.

"Please don't tell me you're wearing that thing in the sun! Just a sec, I'll get you a menu."

"Thanks, April," Trinity said.

April served the seated customers, working her way around the small tables. Her soft Texas accent and cover-girl good looks lent charm to the place.

Trinity drank a glass of the cold water and poured another while quickly glancing at the menu. Other than prices, the place was the same as it had been when it first opened.

"So how are things, Frank?" Lesley slid a chair next to Trinity's. "Don't get up."

The sun on the veranda created highlights in Lesley's sun-streaked blonde hair.

When Lesley bought the Presidio Market, she saved it from the wrecking ball. The previous owner's plan called for a covered multi-level parking garage on a site where Pancho Villa himself once ate lunch. In honor of its historical significance, Lesley put pictures of the revolutionary in the bathroom.

The Presidio Market attracted downtown professionals during the lunch hours and a hodge-podge of students and tourists at night. Lots of people passed through the place.

It wasn't such a longshot that either Lesley or April might have seen Lisa Brooks.

Trinity held up the two photos of Lisa. "Somebody is telling me she hangs out with some frat-rats. Omega House, if that makes a difference. Ever seen her?"

"I've never seen her," Lesley said, "but I know the guys from that house. They come here sometimes. Stoned to the gills. They never have girls with them. What girl would hang around them?"

She looked at the picture more closely. "She's missing?"

"Not really," Trinity said. He knew he would find her. Not much about the case seemed very tricky. Chances were good she was at the frat. Stoned out of her mind, maybe, but not missing.

April came out to the veranda and motioned to

Lesley.

They were both good looking women. That much was undeniable. Trinity remembered a particularly idiotic statement made by Sergeant Kilkenny. It had been in Korea, and Kilkenny had been in the midst of a bleary drunk.

Kilkenny said any good looking woman could either be classified as a Betty or Veronica.

Of course, Kilkenny had been drunk, but his earnestly simplistic statement stayed with Trinity.

Betty or Veronica?

Marilyn Monroe or Elizabeth Taylor?

All-American blonde or exotic brunette?

Of course, Trinity thought, Valerie had been the definition of exotic.

April's back was turned to Trinity. She was taking an order from a customer at a nearby table. Her red apron was tied behind the white blouse she wore above her jeans.

Was April an All-American brunette?

He glanced at Lesley.

Did that make Lesley an exotic blonde?

It made for pleasant speculation.

A CARDBOARD CLOCK

Livingston's body lay at an angle. His arms were thrown back and his head twisted to the side. His blood had dried into a corona on his already dirty white shirt.

Edison felt his eyes start to swim and his legs go weak. He staggered forward, leaned over, and put his hand on Livingston's neck.

As if there would be a pulse.

Nothing.

Edison put his hands on the shoulders of his older brother. In spite of all obstacles, and despite his faults, Livingston had raised him. Put him on a horse, a broomstick first, then a pony, and taught him how to rope.

Now he was dead. A corpse on the floor of a flop-house.

Murdered.

Edison got up from his haunches and looked around the maelstrom of the room. Everything was wrecked, smashed, on its side, as if a tornado had gone through the place. He pieced his way through the debris and went to the bathroom and leaned over the toilet. The vomit came quickly and came back just as fast.

And questions.

A flood of questions.

What should he do?

That was the first question.

Of course the room had no phone.

The sun hit Edison coming out of the door from the tomb-like room.

The motel office was closed.

Edison felt the glass move as he slapped the windowpane.

No answer.

The cardboard clock hanging inside the door indicated that management would be out until one.

He thought about the U-Totem down the street where he'd bought coffee and whiskey.

It seemed like hours ago instead of the few minutes which had passed.

Edison ran out to the curb. The store was way past the place with the VW van mounted on top of a post.

He would need the truck, but he didn't want to leave Livingston.

Edison went back in the motel room and yanked the blue spread from the top of the unmade bed. Slung it over his brother's body then kneeled down and tucked it around Livingston's shoulders.

Livingston used to do that for Edison when he'd been a little boy and had just gone to live with Livingston and Tasha.

The terrible thought hit him when he pulled the truck out of the motel.

What if they think I killed him?

Why wouldn't they?

His fingerprints were in the room, and not much else to go on.

They would ask him where he'd been last night, after he left the campfire.

Where had he gone?

Who saw him there?

Wouldn't they just assume he'd done it?

Edison pounded the steering wheel. He needed to think straight. He didn't even know where the police station was in this town.

The leather-faced U-Totem clerk recognized Edison.

"Back so soon?" the man said.

"I gotta find a cop," Edison said.

He could barely talk. The floor of the U-Totem was starting to spin and he felt like he was going to puke again.

"My brother's been murdered."

AMBER BEADS AND A CONCHO BELT

Trinity stood above Meredith's desk. Looking up at him, her familiar dark eyes danced beneath half-glasses.

"You couldn't possibly have found a busier day to ask for these?"

Trinity leaned forward. "I'd use any excuse to see you, Meredith, you know that."

He meant it, of course. In a way.

In a way he still loved Meredith. Just not in the same way he had years before.

Trinity had climbed the steps to the third floor of the administration building, going directly to Meredith's cubicle, side-stepping the motionless line of slack-jawed students clutching their drop-add forms. The first thing in the morning, the first summer session barely started, and the line already snaked around the bottom floor and out the door into the blazing heat.

"You know I'm just doing this because I love you, Frank." She gave him the smile he knew so well, and the slightest of winks.

At one time, Meredith's face kept Trinity from sleeping at night. He first saw her in a line similar to the one he had just passed through. They were both freshmen standing next to Bear Down Gym. He could have sworn he was standing next to Linda Ronstadt. He had picked up a card for the first class he saw her sign up for and found himself committed for a semester to a nutrition class in the Home Economics building.

Maybe it was an early version of the tennis hustle, but he did meet her.

They held hands while watching Rashomon at the New Loft and kissed on a bench next to the fountain in front of Old Main. They took turns telling each other about their futures, sketchy about the parts the other would play, each knowing they were barely starting their respective first acts.

Today, Meredith wore an elegant string of amber beads and a Guatemalan blouse. A concho belt cinched her slender waist.

Definitely, Meredith was an exotic brunette.

And married. For how many years now?

Trinity remembered the way her body felt on a warm fall evening. Not so long ago? A lifetime ago.

She handed a sheaf of photocopied papers to Trinity.

She still looked like Linda Ronstadt and she still made his senses come to life.

"Your friend signed up for fifteen hours during the spring, but she withdrew from them all. No reason given. Sorry, can't chat."

Meredith waved in the direction of the line.

Where was her wedding ring?

Not on either hand.

The line didn't move. Two girls standing behind Trinity were disgusted with a math teacher. Trinity did a double take. One of the girls, a blonde, looked like the picture of Lisa he took from the sorority house.

Meredith put her ringless hand on top of his and fixed her eyes upon him.

"As usual, Mr. Trinity, any knowledge of your mission will be disavowed."

They both laughed.

In his heart, Trinity knew he would do anything for her.

Leaving, Trinity heard one of the girls start to explain her problem to Meredith.

"And he doesn't even explain anything," the girl said. "He just puts problems up on the board."

Some problem, Trinity thought.

He grabbed a copy of the school directory from a stack as he walked past the girl.

Some problem.

Try finding a missing blonde on this campus.

THE LONG EXPANSE OF NOTHING

Edison had missed the rodeo.

Turning south in the high desert between Holbrook and Snowflake, Edison heard his brother's voice.

The Holbrook police had told him he was free to go. They took his statement at the station. The officer interviewing him knew Tasha. Knew Tasha and Livingston. Hadn't said anything, but Edison read surprise in the officer's eyes. Guys like Livingston usually don't live long.

Livingston and Tasha had taken Duane and him in when Edison's mother died. That had been so long ago Edison couldn't even remember her. All he had for a memory was imagination and a couple of drugstore photo booth snapshots of a pretty woman holding Edison as a baby.

Livingston could ride a bull and tell a story like

nobody else. Edison always looked forward to the stories of the bar fights and rodeos, and later in the evening in the glow of a campfire, tales of the spirit world.

And pulling past Woodruff, just south of Holbrook, Edison heard his brother's voice, as clearly as if Livingston were in the next seat.

As clear as the midnight broadcast from KNDN.

As clearly as Hamlet heard the ghost of his father.

A bull had rolled on Livingston in a rodeo at Indian Wells. The injuries aged Livingston, leaving him a decrepit old man way before his time.

And his drinking increased. Tasha said the doctors had never provided a pain management tool for Livingston more effective than Livingston found in a bottle of Ten High.

Edison paid less and less attention to Livingston's stories which had become bizarre. Livingston took to going out into the desert. He told Edison he saw visions there, and Edison had laughed.

"You're crazy, man."

Edison remembered the look of disappointment on Livingston's face when he'd said that.

And then Edison went east on a scholarship to Dartmouth leaving Tasha to look out after his older brother and his visions.

Edison remembered the look Livingston gave him when he returned from Hanover, still limping from his own surgery, hauling his clothes in a surplus army duffel bag.

"Show me some respect, Little Brother."

For the first time Edison could remember, Livingston was serious with him, and it made Edison angry.

What did respect have to do with anything?

And what was there about Livingston to respect?

But those were the words Edison heard the voice of his older brother say in the F-150, heading south from Holbrook.

"Show me some respect, Little Brother."

It was eerie. It was almost as if Livingston was sitting in the passenger seat.

Edison pulled the truck over onto the wide dirt side of the road.

A cattle fence protected the long expanse of nothing.

He looked both ways. The sun was still high. He made a u-turn and drove the truck back over the long highway toward Holbrook.

AN ORCHESTRA OF MAUVE

Trinity ordered a double shot of espresso at the counter of the downstairs cafe in the student union. He paid the woman at the register and grabbed two packets of sugar. Espresso wasn't on the menu when Trinity went to school.

Compared to the coffee served at the Presidio Market, the espresso was mud.

He took the paper cup to an unoccupied table out of earshot of the morning television talk show and unfolded Lisa's transcript.

She did well in her freshmen courses. In her second semester she signed up for a course on comparative religions and an upper division philosophy class. Her grades were good for these courses and for those held in the fall of her sophomore year. She dropped all her classes in the spring. The transcript listed Lisa's address as the sorority house.

She asked her father for money for summer

school, but hadn't finished her spring classes.

Trinity crumpled his paper cup and threw it in the trash as he left.

✳ ✳ ✳

It took less than fifteen minutes to get from the university up Broadway to the El Encanto home of Arlene Fowler.

London Calling boomed from Trinity's speakers.

Pamela, the sorority advisor, liked jazz. Trinity's tastes were varied.

Lisa's mother lived with her current husband in a large, elegant, white brick house. Two palm trees and a red Cadillac stood sentry on a circular driveway.

Trinity pulled in front of a FOR SALE BY OWNER sign. A hand-lettered note stapled underneath gave a description of the house and the asking price.

"If this price is not in your range," the note read, "please do not waste your time or ours."

Arlene Fowler stood in the doorway, a formidable woman in a pleated white tennis skirt over long bronzed legs. She would be a few years younger than her ex-husband.

Probably closer to my age, Trinity thought. It almost made him shudder.

"Edward said that you would either call or come up. Frankly, I expected you to call first."

Exasperation in her voice mixed with frigid

condescension.

Mrs. Fowler and Edward Brooks would have had some swinging times together in the years before they split up. Mixed doubles before cocktails, and maybe afterwords as well. The drink and the glass she held in her hand was identical to the one Brooks held throughout his interview with Trinity. His and her tumblers. Monogrammed glass. It must have been a struggle splitting up the set. Trinity wondered if the couple had tried any kind of reconciliation. The idea was sadistically appealing.

Mrs. Fowler's current husband might have something to say about that. The doctor might not object. There was as much human warmth in Arlene Fowler as might be found in a glass of frozen gin. Marriage to her would be like mating with a black widow spider. Enjoy the first kiss, baby, because the kicks won't last.

"Frankly, Mr. Trinity, I am appalled that Edward didn't voice his concern before this." Her metallic words were chosen carefully.

Twice she had said "frankly."

"He probably didn't want to upset you," Trinity said. "He wants to believe that nothing's wrong."

"Nothing! How can you stand there and say that my daughters' disappearance is nothing?"

Trinity's temper flashed.

"That's not what I said, Mrs. Fowler. How long has it been since you saw Lisa?"

"My God," she said. "My daughter has vanished

from the face of the earth and Edward in his infinitely childish way has sent you?"

She gave Trinity a withering look as if he was a manifestation of her former husband.

"Honey," a man's voice said, "Who's out there with you?"

Meek. The voice of a small and sad man.

Arlene glared in the direction of the of the voice.

It was a shame, Trinity thought. A shame and a waste. She should have been gorgeous. Her body was as well-constructed and maintained as a luxury sedan, but rage and resentment contorted and crowed out any real claim to beauty.

"Would you say that it's been weeks since you've seen her? Months?"

"George and I saw her at Christmas." Mrs. Fowler looked over her shoulder into the house. "Excuse me," she said. "I'm probably killing the messenger. Would you care to step inside?"

What is it about gin and tonics? Trinity wondered. Both Brooks and his former wife were capable of complete changes of temperament in a matter of seconds.

Arlene Fowler was smiling now. Her version of the perfect hostess. She wouldn't have looked out of place at Lisa's sorority.

Sitting on a long mauve couch, Trinity looked around the living room. It wasn't just the couch. The place was an orchestra of mauve.

He took a glass of water from Mrs. Fowler.

Unlike her ex-husband, she added ice to Trinity's glass. The water was as cold as the room and Arlene Fowler's demeanor.

Through a plate-glass window, Trinity saw a pool surrounded by river rock and native grasses. Life in a well-tended desert. An expensive reproduction of a riparian eco-system long since gone. He half expected a saber-toothed tiger to emerge from the shrubbery.

Noticing his glance, Mrs. Fowler placed herself between Trinity and the window. "You wouldn't believe the wildlife George and I see through here."

A nature lover. Trinity wouldn't have guessed it. He wondered where her tan lines stopped.

Wildlife.

Her breasts were as well defined under tennis togs as those of a chromed mannequin. Did plastic surgeons make house calls to El Encanto?

"Had Lisa changed in any way when you last saw her?"

"I'm not sure what you mean by that, Mr. Trinity. After all, the girl is only nineteen years old. She changes practically every time that we see her."

The girl.

To her mother, Lisa was "the girl."

To her father she was "the most precious thing."

"I mean, did she seem preoccupied in any way? Was she unusually happy or sad?"

"I should tell you this, Mr. Trinity," Arlene

Fowler placed a hand against the plate glass window. One hand on the window, the other vamping her drink above her hip. "My relationship with my daughter is not the strongest."

She's posing for me, Trinity thought. A femme fatale. Barbara Stanwyck, maybe? Knock off her dentist husband for the insurance settlement? He wouldn't put it past her. She stood close enough for Trinity to detect a three-way battle between perfume, gin, and vermouth. A pitched battle with no front-runner.

The estrangement from Lisa didn't surprise him. No other female could survive in this woman's nest. Arlene Fowler's eyes glimmered as she looked at Trinity. And then just as quickly glanced toward the door to another room. A dark haired Barbara Stanwyck, anyway.

"For some reason, Lisa has always blamed me for the divorce. Having her here occasionally is about all that George and I can manage." She nodded again toward the other room. "Frankly, Lisa is less than respectful toward George."

Frankly.

Again.

"She's never accepted George as a father, although he's made more than an effort. Heaven only knows we have tried including her in our circle, but she dismisses any social offering out of hand. It simply was easier for all concerned to have her live up there with her father."

Shaking her head.

"Edward and his paintings."

"Has he always been an artist?"

"Oh, I suppose you might say that. Once upon a time he thought he had talent."

She dipped a crimson fingernail into her drink and stirred.

"Of course you might just as easily call him a professional dilettante. He's never actually worked a day in his life. When I met him, he'd just finished a little stint on the Left Bank. He's long on conversation and short on sales. You may have noticed."

Trinity's mind drifted.

Barbara Stanwyck was a blonde...

He inhaled abruptly.

Arlene Fowler withdrew her finger from her drink and put it next to her lips. "Not that filthy lucre makes any difference to Edward. His auntie left him very well taken care of."

Trinity remembered the swirls on the paintings at Edward Brooks' house. Van Gogh sold only one painting before he died, so Brooks was at least in good company.

"That's Edward's situation?"

Mrs. Fowler looked at Trinity as if he were a slow-witted child.

"Of course it is. How do you think he keeps himself in penny loafers? Certainly not by the sweat of his brow."

"Does Lisa think you caused the divorce?"

"Mr. Trinity, I think that your questions

are getting off the topic. Frankly, the word impertinent comes to mind." She sipped at her drink with all the satisfaction of a cat licking at a saucer. Trinity would have sworn he saw her wink at him.

"And I think so too." Dr. Fowler came out from the other room.

It was an explanation for Arlene Fowler's periodic glances at the door.

The dentist cometh.

Doctor Fowler was a short man. Shorter than Edward Brooks, but sharing with his predecessor an air of inconsequence.

Arlene must find the quality appealing, Trinity thought.

He was at least four inches shorter than his wife. She would tower over him in heels.

"I've heard your entire conversation," Fowler said. "And I must say I agree with my wife. I've got half a mind to throw you out of this house right now."

He let his words hang in the air as if to let Trinity absorb their meaning.

Trinity waited. The two of them made an interesting couple. The doctor made the threats and his wife looked capable of carrying them out.

But somehow, Trinity guessed, Arlene wouldn't throw him out immediately.

Fowler continued. "However," he said, "I am also concerned with Lisa's well-being. For your information, there could be no reason on earth for

Lisa to blame her mother for the divorce. Ed Brooks simply placed Arlene in an impossible situation and she left." Dr. Fowler smiled at his wife. "It really was the only thing for her to do."

He gave a proprietary look toward his wife. "Refill?"

The threat to kick Trinity out was an idle one.

Dr. Fowler was a windbag.

Arlene Fowler nodded, holding a nearly empty glass toward her husband. Fowler hurried off to perform his duty.

"So there wasn't any reason for Lisa to think that you were the cause of the divorce?"

"None whatsoever." She fumbled with the clasp of a gilded box next to Trinity. She pulled out a cigarette and lighted it. "Excuse me, I'm afraid this is rather a more painful subject than I thought it would be. You probably think I'm horrible."

She faced Trinity.

Horrible is a strong word, Trinity thought.

"I've done what I thought was best for the girl. I've seen far too many children fought over by their parents like a trophy in a tug-of-war. I resolved that I wouldn't let that happen to Lisa even if it meant sacrificing myself." Mrs. Fowler paused to exhale, letting the nobility of her inattention sink in.

"I know she hates me. I can't blame her for that. I only wish she could know how much I really care about her. I'm sorry, but I've never really been able to show my affection toward the girl."

The situation called for tears, but Arlene Fowler's eyes were as dry as serpent's scales.

"I'm sorry," she said. "I'm no use at all. I'm sorry."

Dr. Fowler returned with his wife's drink.

Trinity stood up and stepped toward the door. "Mrs. Fowler, it's possible Edward's over-reacting. Let's hope so. She could call up tonight and wonder why everyone is so upset. Believe me though. Ed's just as worried as you are."

"I'm frightened for her."

"I imagine you would be.

"Keep me informed?"

"I'll call you when I find her."

Dr. Fowler spoke.

"You're right, Mr. Trinity. I've told Arlene that Lisa is just playing a little game."

His pink face spoke earnest sincerity.

"She'll come home when the money runs out."

That could take a while, Trinity thought.

He turned to leave. Arlene Fowler stepped nearer to him. Her husband had retreated to the back room.

"I may have come on a little strong," she said. "I didn't mean to."

Trinity shook his head.

"It's all right."

She looked at him for a long time.

"Call me anyway," she said.

Trinity opened the door.

"I'll call when I have news about Lisa."

THE SPIRES OF MONUMENT VALLEY

What was I thinking? Edison wondered. Why did I drive away like that?

If nothing else, Tasha needed him.

The cops hadn't let him go back to the motel.

He was in his F-150 on his way to see her.

Edison hoped they hadn't let her go to the motel, either. She didn't need that.

The truck stop's diner was a stylized hogan, oversized with enormous murals showing semis driving against the spires of Monument Valley.

Tasha's eyes were red. She stood on her tiptoes to give Edison a kiss as he walked in.

Debbie was still there. She glanced, heavy-eyed, at Edison.

Tasha's started to cry. "I got a phone call," she said, straightening her white apron. "Duane."

Edison could tell that it hurt Tasha to say the name of his younger brother. It made him angry. More than angry.

What had the boy ever brought into the family except shame and sadness?

Edison looked carefully at Tasha. She was a good woman. She had worked hard and deserved better than the treatment she got from Duane.

Livingston had been enough of a burden, but Tasha had married him and stayed with him.

Tasha had always treated Duane like her own son.

"What did he want?"

Tasha drew in her breath and stared at Edison.

"Duane knows who killed Livingston."

REAR-VIEW MIRROR

Wendy Chandler's home was not nearly as well cared for as the others on the one-way street bordering the Sam Hughes Neighborhood. The walls were cracked stucco. No paint had touched the place in years.

Trinity wondered if talking to Arlene Fowler had been necessary. It probably was, he decided. Some things a phone call could not reveal. Edward Brooks might have his faults as a father, but Trinity could see why Lisa would prefer him to her mother.

Black widow spiders like Arlene Fowler weren't renowned for their maternal instincts.

Wendy answered the doorbell quickly. She was older than Trinity expected. Her streaked honey-blonde hair was cut in a shag and a partially unbuttoned white shirt exposed the top of a turquoise brassiere.

Straightening the hem of her narrow black silk

skirt she motioned Trinity to step into the house. "You caught me," she said. "I was just heading to work."

Wendy gave off an aura of pure sex.

"Pamela Chambers said that you might know something about Lisa Brooks. Her father's worried about her."

Wendy pulled a lipstick from her handbag and stood in front of the large gold-framed mirror in the doorway.

"Sorry," she said. "I'm in such a hurry. I don't know if I can help you."

"You haven't seen Lisa since..."

"God, for a while anyway, I guess. I wondered about her too, to be honest."

The room was furnished sparsely with a recliner and a drop-cloth covered couch. Indentations in the carpet marked where other furniture had been.

"Lisa was acting strangely. She and Billy."

"Who's Billy?"

"Billy's one of the boys from the Omega House."

Wendy pursed her lips and looked at them from another angle before applying more lipstick.

"He's not that bad. He's even kind of cute."

"When did you see her last?"

"I left right after finals."

She turned toward Trinity and teased her fingernails through her hair. "God... Her father asked you to find her? He must be worried."

"Have you seen her since spring break?"

Wendy's face was a cipher. A quick shrug. A peek backward toward the mirror.

"When would you say that you last saw her?"

The flippant look disappeared from Wendy's face.

Briefly.

"I'm not sure," she said. "In a way I didn't care. I was glad that she was gone."

Wendy put her hands up. Fanned the air.

"It's all right," Trinity said. "I wasn't asking…"

"Some friend I am. But Lisa got so weird. Ask anyone."

"Weird in what way?"

"Just weird. All this Indian stuff. She took it all so seriously."

Wendy glanced at her watch. "God… I'm so late…"

From the Bronco, Trinity watched Wendy get into a dented red convertible and adjust her rear-view mirror. A minute passed before the convertible pulled away from the curb..

Wendy was either watching Trinity or checking her makeup.

Trinity would have put money on the makeup.

A BLOOD-RED CONCRETE FLOOR

The Omega house lawn was a scorched tangle of dead summer weeds. One lighted match away from a brushfire. Minutes after talking to Wendy Chandler, Trinity pulled into the nearly empty driveway and parked next to the only other vehicle, a stripped-down Ford Fairlane with expired tags.

Nobody answered Trinity's knock. The carved wooden door was slightly ajar.

He pushed it open.

The Omega house was as dark as the basement of a mausoleum.

Trinity's eyes adjusted gradually to the dim light.

The living room was furnished with tired couches and a television chained to the wall. An impressive place if your taste ran to dissolution.

It was as different from the sorority as Jekyll was from Hyde. Trinity understood why Pamela Chambers was repelled by this collegiate skid row. The back of the house was a dining hall. Concrete floor painted blood-red. A long table covered with dried ketchup and flies. In the kitchen, a cockroach scuttled over a counter of abandoned dishes, pots and pans.

Trinity hummed "La Cucaracha."

On a cork message board a torn piece of paper with a scrawled message.

> Billy Loves Lisa

Two wings of the fraternity house branched out from the living room. Two wings, Trinity thought. Like Robert Frost. Two wings diverged from this crummy room, and sorry I could not... Footsteps clomped along the upstairs hallway and Trinity heard a toilet flush. A shower started and lasted forever.

A kid wearing a turned-around ballcap walked down the staircase toweling. Wearing sunglasses in the darkened living room.

Trinity stood in the center of the living room. The kid scratched his bare stomach, an unlit cigarette dangling from his lips.

"Hey," the kid said.

"Are you Billy?"

The kid reached into the pocket of his shorts and pulled out a book of paper matches.

"What the fuck are you doing here," the kid said.

"I'm looking for Billy. Who are you?"

Trinity stepped in front of the kid, blocking the kitchen entrance.

The kid held his cigarette between the thumb and forefinger of his right hand.

"Name's Mark."

If Mark planned to eat anything from the kitchen, Trinity would be doing him a favor by keeping him out. The place was ptomaine waiting to happen.

Mark walked around Trinity and picked up a bowl from the counter. Sprayed it with a jet of water.

Satisfied with the hygienic procedure, he pulled a box of cereal from above the sink.

"Billy's not here. You his dad?"

"Friend of the family. Is he around? I need to give him something."

"You can leave it here. I don't know when he'll be back."

"Who's Lisa?"

"What do you mean?" Mark propped his sunglasses on the top of his cap.

He squinted at Trinity through bloodshot eyes.

"I saw the note. Billy loves Lisa." Trinity pointed toward the corkboard. "Who's Lisa?"

"Oh that Lisa." Mark shook his head. "They broke up. It's been a while. I haven't seen her for a long time."

"How long is long?"

Mark wasn't bothering with milk. He shoveled down his cereal and poured another bowl.

"How should I know? What's it to you?"

Trinity moved inside the kitchen door. The place smelled like stale beer, cigarette smoke, and urine.

"Is that your car out there?"

Mark nodded his head.

"A '65?"

Another nod.

A real outgoing kid, Trinity thought. A real public speaker. He would look better with his face rearranged.

There was something irritating about him.

Everything.

"Good car for the desert."

Trinity pulled a card from his pocket.

"Here, let me give you this."

Keeping his patience wasn't easy.

"If Billy shows up, tell him to give me a call. That goes for Lisa, too. It's important."

Mark looked from the card to Trinity.

Then back at the card.

"This is you?"

"That's me."

Along with his eloquence, the kid had a genius for grasping the obvious. Who else would be handing out Trinity's card in the maggot-infested dump?

"You know you were asking about Billy?"

"Yeah?"

Mark put the cereal bowl down on the counter. A roach scuttled out of a coffee cup.

"I wouldn't count on seeing Billy for a while. He's locked up."

"He's in jail?"

Mark shook his head. Took another handful of cereal.

"No, he freaked out."

"What do you mean?"

More cereal.

"Somebody said they put him in the nut ward. Nobody's seen him for a while. He was out on Speedway, naked."

Trinity nodded.

Mark shrugged. "Kind of fucked-up, huh?"

"Was this before or after he broke up with Lisa?"

"Oh man... How would I know that? Was I supposed to be keeping track?"

Mark's cynical bravado had returned. He pulled a cigarette from a twisted pack of Kools.

"Look," he said, "I'll keep your card, man."

He offered his hand to Trinity, and after breaking the grip, quickly pulled it away and snapped his fingers. A real hep-cat, Trinity thought. Born too late for the Beat Generation.

The two stood in the entryway by the mailboxes. Trinity peered at the mostly empty cubbyholes.

"Anything in here for Billy? I can take it for

him."

Mark fell for the ruse. He put his hand in the box marked B. Carton.

"Not a thing."

Trinity paused in front of a composite picture by the front door. Billy Carton, second row, far left. A blank expression.

Mark watched Trinity leave.

"Lemme know if you hear anything."

Trinity looked back.

"No problemo," he said.

THE PUZZLE'S BLUE SKY

Finding Billy was easy. The county hospital switchboard operator said he had been admitted in the morning. The psychiatric nurse took a break from knitting to talk to Trinity.

"You're what relationship?" she said, peering at Trinity.

"Friend of the family," Trinity said.

The nurse shook her head.

"Billy was in terrible shape when he come to us. Extremely psychotic." She rustled in her bag for another skein of yarn. "He'll definitely need to stay on his meds, if you could help with that."

Billy slouched over a card table wearing a T-shirt, a pair of blue jeans, and an even more blank expression than he'd shown in the fraternity composite. Five hundred jigsaw puzzle pieces spread out in front of him. Only a patch of sky and one arm of a windmill emerged from chaos.

Trinity sat opposite Billy at the card table.

The nurse kept knitting. Billy looked out over an invisible landscape. Trinity leaned forward and whispered.

"Billy, my name is Frank Trinity. I need your help."

No response. Billy looked at a piece of the puzzle.

"Lisa needs your help too, Billy."

Billy looked up at Trinity as if seeing him for the first time. "Are you a card player?"

"Billy," Trinity continued, "Lisa's father is looking for her. Do you know where she is?"

Billy stared at Trinity.

"You have gunfighter eyes."

"We can't figure out where Lisa's been the last week or so."

Trinity picked up one of the five hundred puzzle pieces.

A piece of blue sky.

"Her father's worried."

Billy shook his head.

"Ask Parrot."

"Parrot?"

"Yeah. He'll know where she is."

"Who's Parrot?"

"Parrot."

Billy looked perplexed. He pointed at the back of the day room.

"Did you come in through there?"

Trinity shook his head.

"I came in through the front door."

"That makes sense," Billy said. "You're a gunfighter."

Trinity snapped in the piece of the puzzle. Only four hundred and eighty or so pieces remained. Enough to keep Billy occupied.

"You're getting out of here today?"

It seemed impossible.

"Maybe."

"When did you see Lisa?"

"I told you. Ask Parrot. I haven't seen her."

Trinity leaned forward across the table.

"Don't mess with me, Billy. I'm in a hurry. How much acid did you take?"

"Acid?" The question offended Billy. A trace of a frown crept across his face.

"I wouldn't take acid. It's unnatural."

Trinity got up. Billy was too far gone to give any meaningful information.

"I'll see you around, Billy. Don't take any wooden nickels."

Trinity stepped toward the door.

"Hey..." Billy said. He put his forefinger over his lips and motioned for Trinity.

Trinity put his ear down to Billy's cupped mouth.

Billy's voice was small, but the words were unmistakable.

"Can you get me out of here?"

The nurse smiled at Trinity as he walked past her.

"Will you be the one picking Billy up?"

"I believe Bill's made other arrangements."

The nurse nodded.

"Somebody will need to..."

Billy, still staring at Trinity, pantomimed the slow-draw of an invisible gun.

"Be seeing you, Shane."

THE QUANAH PARKER THING

Edison stared at Duane.

Tasha's living room was tidy. Framed studio pictures of Livingston, Edison, and Duane hung above the brown couch where Duane was sprawled.

It was late in the afternoon. Shadows from the barred window fell across the stubble on Duane's shaved head.

Duane refused to look at his brother.

He might as well be in prison, Edison thought. That's where he's heading.

"You tell me everything, Duane."

"Shit... I was stoned," Duane said. He held his face in his hands.

Edison pulled his chair closer to Duane.

"Don't give me any bullshit excuses. I need to know everything."

"It was the buttons, man..." Duane looked up at Edison as if this explained everything.

Livingston had used peyote for years. Always, he claimed, for sacred purposes.

Livingston had the whole Quanah Parker thing down.

Edison had never been sure if his older brother's use of the plant really was as spiritual as he claimed.

But really, with Livingston cold and dead, what did it matter now?

Edison leaned down and put his face closer to his younger brother.

"What are you talking about?"

"I told this white guy..." Duane could barely complete the words. "I told this greasy piece of shit about Livingston."

"Who? Where?"

"This guy shows up, looking for Livingston. He was staying... I'd smoked a bowl, so I was a little wasted. He had a tattoo of a parrot on his arm. Said he was from Tucson."

"You told this guy how to find Livingston?"

It was beyond Edison's belief.

"He wanted to score." Duane threw his head back. "Livingston didn't mind selling a few buttons. You know that.

Only the thought of Tasha kept Edison from lifting his brother up by his neck and strangling him.

"You going to tell the cops this?"

Duane stared at his older brother.

"You shitting me? Me? Talk to the cops?"

Edison shook his head.

Duane pointed at Edison. "You're the one. You live in Tucson. Maybe you'll see him."

Edison shook his head again. "What were you saying before?"

"When?"

"You said the guy was living somewhere?"

Duane nodded. "That was the thing. He knew Livingston anyway. The guy had a room at the Sunset. He just wanted to find him."

The Sunset Motel.

That wouldn't give Edison a hell of a lot to work with. Fifteen bucks would get you a room there and no questions asked.

"What else?" Edison clenched his fists and stared at Duane.

"I don't know... Shit." Duane shook his head. "I got a note with the room number..."

"Where?"

Duane dug into his jeans pockets and pulled out his wallet. He sifted through it until he found a folded memo from the A-1 Extermination Company in Tucson.

The note, wadded up and written in a smeared pencil line said Parrot had been living in room seven at the Sunset.

EYES A PALER SHADE OF BLUE

Trinity welcomed the late afternoon sun and the slight breeze after the claustrophobic interior of the mental ward. The place had reeked of pine-sol.

He was hungry. Dealing with Billy took a toll on Trinity. A dark veil of futility shrouded him.

The Presidio Market was less than a five minute drive from the hospital.

Lesley seated him on the veranda.

"Thank you, sweetie," Trinity heard the woman at the next table say as Lesley put the menus down on the table. "By the way," the woman said, "I think your hair coloring is simply fabulous."

Lesley touched Trinity on the arm. Trinity nodded and glanced around the room. The cheery atmosphere felt good after the psych ward.

"You haven't found her yet?"

Lesley put her hand on Trinity's neck, her thumb rubbing under his collar.

"Not yet. I could be overlooking something."

He could be overlooking a lot of things. Obvious things. But Trinity had a bedrock belief in persistence. Lesley worked her hand further down his neck and her nails scratched his back. "Do you think she's still around here?"

"She's got to be," Trinity said. "I think she's staging a minor rebellion. Her folks broke up and she's never forgiven her mother."

Even as he said it, his own words sounded simplistic to Trinity. He looked at the menu. "So, she's gotten involved with some real characters."

"The mother?"

"No, sorry, the mother is married to a dentist. Very conventional, you might say. Lisa's hooked up with a frat guy from a place called the Omega House who's managed to fry out his brains."

"The fraternity was the Omega House?"

"The frat house? Right... Lisa's boyfriend is named Billy Carton. Last time I saw him he was wearing blue paper slippers and waiting for lanyard making class. There's another guy too. Somebody named Parrot."

Lesley took her hand from Trinity's back.

"Sorry," Lesley said. "Billy Carton doesn't ring a bell. What happened to him?"

"Who knows," Trinity said. "Too much dope. He burned out his circuits."

"All of them?"

"Maybe not all." Trinity poured a glass of water. "I guess I'll have the pastrami. They're letting him out of the hospital this afternoon."

"In that shape?"

Lesley's eyes were a paler shade of blue in the afternoon light. What had Billy said? He said Trinity had gunfighter eyes. Lesley's eyes were blue. Trinity worked over the two unrelated thoughts. He recalled reading that though many gunfighters had deep set blue eyes, there really was no connection between cold-blooded killing and eye color.

But Lesley's eyes were certainly beautiful. He hadn't payed attention to them before.

"He isn't ready to get out of the hospital," Trinity said.

"So why are they letting him?"

"I'm guessing the insurance only pays so much. After that, it's out on the street." He took a sip of water. "They'll have him doped up."

Lesley stood up. "So who's this Parrot?"

"A guy Billy mentioned. Doesn't ring any bells, does it?

"Not at all," Lesley said, picking up his menu. "I don't know either of them, but I'll keep a lookout."

"Thanks," Trinity said, "I appreciate your help."

She winked at him.

"That's what neighbors are for."

Her eyes were more than beautiful, he thought. They were stunning.

MOMENTO MORI

Billy's home address in the student directory took Trinity near Davis-Monthan Air Force Base. A short man with a face the color of liverwurst, Mr. Carton sipped a can of Schlitz, holding a hose over a patch of gravel. The sod was slightly larger and denser than the surface of a pool table. Carton stood sweating in a polyester short-sleeved shirt. He gave a cursory spray to the rest of his mica flecked mini-plantation when Trinity introduced himself.

"I'm looking for a girl named Lisa Brooks," Trinity said.

Carton held the hose at waist level, soaking the patch again.

"What's that got to do with me?"

"Somebody told me that she was friends with your son."

Trinity held out the picture of Lisa.

Carton shook his head.

"Never seen her before."

"Never?" Trinity said.

What never? Trinity thought.

The old Gilbert and Sullivan routine...

Well, hardly ever.

Carton snorted and shook his head. "Look, I won't pretend this is the first time Billy's had problems."

"But you've never seen the girl?" Trinity believed him. Carton didn't look like a liar, and he didn't look like someone his son would confide in.

Carton played with the spigot before squaring up to Trinity. On his forearm, a blurred tattoo of a dagger pierced a skull. Momento Mori. Remember we will die.

Valerie had taught him the phrase and in her death had taught him its meaning.

"You know what?" Carton said. "Those people down at the hospital called me earlier. You know what they wanted me to do? They wanted me to come down and pick Billy up down there at four o'clock this afternoon."

He turned the spigot to give more attention to a part of the lawn.

"Not just pick him up."

His voice rose in contempt.

"They want me to go into something they call 'family therapy.'"

Carton took a swig from the can of beer and held it against his forehead.

With the beer and the tattoo, he reminded Trinity of Sgt. Kilkenny.

"Family therapy," he repeated. "Do you know where I'm going to be today at four o'clock?"

Trinity didn't know. He suspected it would not be at the county hospital.

"Let me tell you..." Mr. Carton said. "You said your name was what?"

"Trinity."

"Right. Let me tell you where I'll be, Trinity. I'll be right here at my house. That's where I'll be. I'll be having another beer, or watching TV, or I don't know what else. Maybe I'll be checking the air in my tires."

He gave a withering look to Trinity. "I can tell you one place I won't be."

Trinity guessed again.

Not at the hospital.

"I won't be at any lousy hospital listening to some two-bit piece-of-shit shrink tell me what kind of a lousy parent I've been."

It would be interesting, Trinity thought, to know exactly what kind of lousy parent Mr. Carton had been. In his experience, no two were ever the same.

Billy's father was different from Edward Brooks. And both were different from Arlene Fowler.

"Mr. Carton, did Billy ever mention any girls to you?"

"Billy doesn't mention anything to me. That's the truth of it. If we ever speak two sentences that's something."

"Does he talk to Mrs. Carton?"

"His mother lives in Pennsylvania. She ran off."

It was an offhand observation, as if Billy's mother was an unwanted pet.

Mr. Carton turned his attention back to the hose, directing the water toward a bougainvillea shrub snaking its way up the side of the slump-block house.

"The water bill here. You wouldn't believe it."

A small woman appeared at the front door, holding a mop in one hand and a pail in the other.

"Charlie. Come here right now." The woman's voice was mildly strident. "I need you to do something."

"Hey," Mr. Carton said, "duty calls."

He flashed a just-between-us-guys grin at Trinity.

A Kilkenny grin.

"These women catch on quick, don't they?"

Some women, Trinity thought, catch on quicker than others.

NOT A COP

There were three new messages on the machine. Trinity wasted no time punching the button.

Mark. From the fraternity house.

"Hey Trinity," Mark said. "You gave me your card and I need to talk to you. I'm at the house right now. I don't want to talk over the phone."

"Take a number," Trinity said.

April, from the Presidio Market left the second message.

"Lesley told me about the girl you're looking for. I remember a guy with a parrot tattooed on his arm. He's come in a few times. He's pretty nasty. If he's the same guy, he hangs out on Fourth Avenue. I've seen him down there, too."

The last call was from Edward Brooks. Fear had replaced bravado. Brooks was scared.

"Trinity," he said, "I need to see you. I got a message from Lisa."

It was going to be busy. Trinity checked his watch. A quarter past two. If he hurried, he could talk to Mark. He found him on the porch of the Omega House, sunglasses making his features small.

"Do you need a search warrant to look at somebody's room?"

"Police do," Trinity said, "but I don't. I'm not a cop. What do you want?"

If Mark wanted legal advice, he'd come to the wrong man. Trinity knew the answers, but it wasn't his department.

"It's not so much what I need to tell you. I got something to show you, but I don't want to get busted. None of this is my shit."

Trinity followed Mark upstairs. Mark looked over his shoulder at Trinity.

"You're sure you're not a cop?"

Somebody must have fed Mark the fiction that police were obliged to tell the truth when directly asked if they were a law enforcement officer.

Trinity fought the urge to punch the kid.

"Just show me what you need to show me."

Standing in front of the last door in the hall, Trinity could barely see the interior.

The light was dim, for starters. A window at the end of the hall had been blocked out with plywood. Someone had attempted a semi-abstract mural on the wall next to the bathroom. Planets spinning over a roiling sea. The obvious ones, of course. Saturn and Jupiter. The rest were ill-defined and out of proportion. Several open cans of dried paint had been placed on a filthy bed sheet. It was no Edward Brooks. Whoever painted it couldn't decide between planets or seascape. Elements of both were in evidence, the rings of Saturn rendered in fluorescent greens and oranges next to a reddish sea.

"I'm not a cop. I didn't show you a badge, did I?"

Trinity's evasion seemed to reassure Mark.

"I got to thinking that if you were looking for Billy then the cops might be next. That's why I called you. I don't want to be busted for something I didn't have anything to do with."

"I'll tell you the truth, Mark. I wasn't looking for Billy. I'm looking for Lisa."

Trinity shook the handle of the door.

Perhaps the muralist had continued somewhere painting landing crafts, or even little green men.

"It's too bad I wasn't looking for Billy. He was easy to find."

Trinity gave the door two hard knocks.

No answer.

He turned to Mark. This is the room you want me to see?"

Mark nodded.

He looked less confident than he had earlier. He stood next to Trinity, staring at the door. "So, would you be, like, required to show a badge if you were a cop?"

Nervous chit-chat.

Trinity pushed tentatively at the door, assessing its strength. "How would I know, Mark? Why don't you ask a cop?"

"I haven't been in this room," Mark said quickly.

"Why not?"

Mark shifted his feet from one to the other.

"Billy scared me. He scared the shit out of me, really. He was out of his mind. I just stayed away from this part of the house."

"That's his painting?" Nodding at the planets.

Mark nodded.

"Pretty good idea to give a wide berth." Trinity raised his boot and smashed in the door. The frame splintered like kindling under an ax.

He stepped in, followed not too closely by Mark.

They should have been carrying torches. Villagers investigating the haunted manor.

"Billy's room?" Trinity said. "Quite a little opium den."

Two uncovered mattresses lay on the floor on either side of a bedraggled recliner.

That was Billy's furniture, the rest of the room was a lab.

Pots and pans and a propane cooking stove in place of beakers and a Bunsen burner. Trinity sniffed the frying pan resting on one of the burners. He pulled a bandanna from his pocket and grabbed the lid of a long cold dutch oven.

The stench filling the room was not familiar.

A congealed mass of viscous green slime had hardened to rock at the bottom of the pot.

Trinity put the lid down.

"You didn't notice this? Not even the smell?"

"I didn't say that," Mark was defensive. "I just

stayed out of the way. You know, live and let live."

A regular Mahatma Gandhi.

Mark's lips were stretched into a wretched grin.

Trinity flicked the switch of a high intensity light. Billy's marijuana plants needed watering.

The chemistry set had trumped his botany project.

"Hey," Mark said, "am I in trouble?"

A kid, waiting to see the school principal.

"I told you I'm not a cop." Trinity hated disillusioning the kid. "But you could be in trouble. It just depends."

"Depends on what? This isn't my shit. I already told you. I don't know anything about it. Am I going to get busted?"

"Could be," Trinity said, "but not if you're gone." He pointed vaguely to the parking lot. "Does that heap run?"

Mark stared at Trinity.

"Your car. Does it run?"

"Oh man, I was bullshitting you. It's not my car. It's just been parked out there for a while."

"You've got my card, right?"

Mark nodded. A slight turn of his expression. Even frightened, he was still arrogant.

"Let me see it."

Mark pulled out a pack of cigarettes from his shirt. The card lay under the cellophane wrapper. Trinity wrote down the phone number of the Presidio Market on the back. He walked out into the hall, followed by Mark.

"Get all your things together. I guess you'll need to walk. I wouldn't come back here."

He looked at Mark again.

The boy was scared.

Trinity handed the card back.

"If you need to reach me quickly use the number on the back. They know how to get hold of me."

NO DRINK IN HIS HAND

He didn't have a drink in his hand this time.

Edward Brooks tried sounding casual as he greeted Trinity.

"Boy am I glad to…"

Trinity interrupted.

"What time did the call from Lisa come in?"

"It came in before I called you. That was what? Ten? You're a busy man."

"What did she say?"

"She wanted more money. A lot more. She didn't say where she was."

"How much more money?"

"Ten thousand."

"You asked her where she was?"

"Of course I did, but she wouldn't tell me. I almost said that I wouldn't deposit the money."

"It's all right," Trinity said. "You did what you did. She's withdrawn the money?"

"All of it."

"Different locations? You can't take that much out in one spot."

"I wouldn't know. I haven't checked." Brooks was sweating. "Look," he said, "I'm going to have a drink. Care to join me?"

If it was a joke, Trinity wasn't going to respond. A drink.

"Did Lisa sound different? Was there any noise or voices in the background?"

"She sounded like she was in a hurry. She just said she needed the money. No explanation."

"That's unusual?"

"Damn right it's unusual. And it's a lot of money, too."

"What about the background noises?"

"It sounded like a pay phone, but I'm only guessing."

"Put a recorder on the phone. Tape any calls that come in. Keep her talking. Keep asking her where she is. She wants you to send money. Use that."

"I'm sorry," Brooks said. "It sounds calculated."

"It is calculated. To make sure Lisa's safe."

"Well naturally, but…"

"We're trying to get some information. Are you okay with that?"

"Don't get me wrong, Mr. Trinity."

Brooks was rattled. He poured a tall glass of gin and tossed in a handful of ice."

"Lay off the gin, Brooks. You need to be sharp."

"This is how I get sharp and stay sharp, Mr.

Trinity. I don't know any other way."

Brooks saluted Trinity with the glass.

"I'm feeling sharper than when you first walked in. No offense to you."

It was a tall drink. Trinity left Brooks to it.

OUTSIDE THE KASHMIR TEA ROOM

The smell of reefer was strong on Fourth Avenue.

Reefer, patchouli oil and street grime.

The avenue, still a haven for runaways, dogs, and tourists. Still as funky as it had been twenty years before.

Elmore Biggs sat cross-legged in front of the Kashmir Tea Room, he and his dog shaded by an olive tree. He slammed percussion on the battered body of his guitar, scraping a bottleneck over rusted strings. A few coins lay inside Elmore's open guitar case. Elmore kept a dirty yellow joint wedged between the tuning pegs of his guitar, the smoke cascading over his stubby goatee. With baggy purple pants and a leather vest over his bare chest, Elmore could have been an opening act in a Baghdad blues den.

"Trinity, what's happening brother?" Elmore held out his palm.

Trinity skinned Elmore's hand. "Ain't nothing."

Elmore slapped at the guitar strings with the bottleneck.

Trinity fluttered a ten into Elmore's case.

"So where are your girlfriends?"

"Too early for the ladies," Elmore said. "You bring your harp?"

How long ago was that? Trinity wondered. Had it been twenty years? Twenty years since Trinity had jammed with Elmore?

Twenty years, on the same street, but under a different tree.

People had gone to prison for life and returned in half that time.

Somewhere, Trinity had a picture of the two of them. With a Marine Band harmonica, a Pignose amp, and dark glasses, Trinity had looked like a skinny Paul Butterfield outside the Fillmore. Elmore looked about the same as he did today minus the gray hair.

Trinity feigned a tap of his pockets. "Sorry Elmore, didn't bring it today."

Twenty years. That's how long it had been. It occurred to Trinity that Elmore was old.

"Shit, Trinity," Elmore shook his head. "You know that's the only reason I put up with your ass."

Trinity enjoyed listening to and even being the target of Elmore's jive. He leaned over and scratched Elmore's dog behind the ears.

The dog, a black and tan, scratched its appreciation.

"I should have brought it," Trinity shrugged, "but I'm kind of busy. I'm looking for a girl."

Elmore looked up quickly. "What kind of girl you looking for?"

Trinity pulled out a picture of Lisa. The glare of the sun reflected from the glossy paper.

"Have you seen her?"

Elmore took the paper, propped his sunglasses on his forehead and held the picture close.

"You find this on a milk carton?"

"Bottle of Ripple, Elmore. Surprised you don't recognize it."

Elmore handed the picture back. "Should I have seen her?"

"She's missing a while, Elmore. I wonder if she hung around here. You know, one of your legion of admirers."

Elmore laughed. "As always, Trinity, you have come to the right place."

"You've seen her?"

"I see ladies look like her every day."

"How about this one?"

"Easy, Trinity. All things in good time."

Elmore dragged on the joint. Played a riff on the guitar. Richie Havens. *Freedom*.

"Seems to me if we're talking about the same woman, she ain't too particular about the company she keeps."

"Who was she with?"

"Relax, my man. Relax."

Elmore thumped the bottleneck against the guitar. He took another drag from the joint, held in the smoke while slamming a high note on the guitar.

"You should slow down. Meditate or something. Might not even be the same lady."

Trinity put the picture in his shirt pocket and looked at Elmore. Thirty years at least he'd been out here in the sun doing this *Mod Squad* bit.

He should be in the Smithsonian, Trinity thought.

Play along.

"I dig, Elmore."

Elmore pulled out a wooden match from his vest and lit it with his thumbnail. He held the flame up to the roach. Offered it to Trinity.

Trinity shook his head.

Elmore pulled the roach back toward himself and stared at the smoldering remnant.

"This might have been the lady in your picture. Could be some other lady. People look alike in a picture. Know what I'm saying?"

Trinity nodded.

"That's good, Trinity. You know women come down here to soak up the exotic atmosphere. That's what makes this gig so exceptional."

He held his arms out in self-satisfaction.

"I provide atmosphere."

As if Fourth Avenue shopkeepers hired Elmore

to add to the ambiance.

"Look Elmore," Trinity said, "why don't we just suppose she's the same girl? Wouldn't that make things a little less complicated?"

Elmore nodded.

"Sure would, Trinity. Sure would. I'm getting there."

Elmore's dog got up, stretched, walked over to pillar in front of the coffee house and lifted its leg.

All in good time.

"No hurry, Elmore," Trinity said.

"That's better, Trinity. Much better. Seems to me like your young friend here don't pay much attention to the company she keep." Elmore snapped his finger. "Seems to me that she making the scene with a local character."

"Name?"

Elmore gave Trinity a reproachful look.

"Strange dude name Parrot."

"Exactly," Trinity said.

"Trinity. You ever see this dude?"

"Never."

"Well, he ain't a pretty man. Matter of fact you could say that he's stone ugly."

Parrot looked philosophically at the dog.

Of course we both know there are some women who freak for that sort of thing. You just never know."

Trinity shrugged.

"Parrot tattooed on his arm, right?"

"That's him. And a lot of other shit. Got most of

his teeth knocked out."

Elmore shrugged.

"But she was looking good."

"How long ago did you see them?"

"Oh man, you're asking too much for a dime… I might tell Mr. Jackson."

Trinity nodded, pulled out a bill from his wallet and dropped it in the case.

"That's it, Elmore. Buy yourself a sundae."

Elmore grinned, exposing gold in his front teeth.

"That's more like it, Trinity. You know I have a sweet tooth."

Elmore adjusted his sunglasses. Stared at the sky.

"Come to think of it, I may have seen them a week ago. Maybe two."

"How close did they look?"

"Well they was tight, Trinity, if that's what you're asking. But she didn't look too hung up on him. They were driving in that fucked-up car of his."

"You think she wanted to be with him?"

"How the hell would I know that?"

"What do you know about this guy?"

"Parrot?"

"Exactly. Where does he live? Where does he spend his time. That kind of thing."

"Well it ain't like I'm tight with the dude."

"I understand."

"Fact is, I probably haven't seen him more than

three or four times. You know what I'm saying?"

Trinity nodded.

"He works at that extermination place down by the underpass."

Trinity looked down the street. The underpass was about three blocks away.

"Thanks a lot, Elmore. It was for a good cause." Trinity paused. "That fucked-up car... was it a Fairlane?"

Elmore shook his head.

"Now how the hell would I remember what kind of car it was?"

Trinity nodded.

Elmore was right. Why would Elmore take the time to remember something like that? He started to walk back toward the Bronco.

Elmore's voice stopped him.

"One other thing about this dude."

"What's that?"

No grin from Elmore this time.

"Watch your ass, Trinity. This fucking Parrot is crazy."

A-1 EXTERMINATION COMPANY

The A-1 Extermination Company stood by the underpass separating Fourth Avenue from downtown Tucson. Corrugated steel doors baked in the sun. Frayed handbills plastered along the side of the building advertised a reggae festival and a solar convergence. A sun-bleached blue Volkswagen was parked on the side of the building.

A musty odor greeted Trinity inside the place. Rows of folding tables were heaped with cardboard boxes. Mismatched supermarket china, toaster ovens, eight-track tapes.

Trinity fished a dusty meat grinder from a whiskey box.

"Help you?" A man wearing an Hawaiian shirt came out of an office area. His black slacks and two-toned loafers could have been salvaged from one of the boxes.

"I hope you can." Trinity handed the man a card. "I'm looking for a guy. Are you the boss?"

"Name's Jennings. Ralph Jennings."

"The guy I'm looking for is named Parrot. Do you know him?"

Ralph Jennings whistled.

"Do I know him?" He motioned to Trinity. "Have a seat," he said. "Sorry about the clutter."

Clutter wasn't the word, Trinity thought. Jennings' office went way beyond a few misplaced items.

A bomb had exploded in the room and someone tried tidying it with a fan. The place was a display of pathological hoarding instincts.

"No problem," Trinity said.

He stepped over a water-streaked box marked MENS MAGS '60 - '63.

"Parrot works here?"

"Worked," Jennings said, "if you want to call it that. Last couple of weeks, I should have fired him."

"What was his job?"

Jennings pointed into his office.

"He set appointments. To tell you the truth, he was good at it when he hadn't been drinking too much. I don't mind a little, but..."

"When did you see him last?"

"It's been a few days. My wife does payroll so you could check with her."

"So it's been at least a week?"

"Give or take," Jennings said. "Could have been

longer. But if he hadn't stopped showing up, I was going to fire him anyway. Too bad. He wasn't bad when he started. Got him from a casual agency. I was going to work him into the route. He could have done good." Jennings sounded wistful. "Parrot was a hustler. I'll give him that."

"What changed?"

"I'd say a bunch of things. First of all, you never knew if he'd come in or not. You know, I've got to be able to count on a man being here. If I don't get appointments, the whole operation is shot."

"Do you know how I can get in touch with him?"

"Hey, I've told you what I know. I could probably find his application if you give me a minute." He started looking around the room. "Tell you the truth, the guy always seemed a little nuts to me."

"How so?"

Jennings looked at Trinity.

"Well, maybe that's a little too strong a description. I'll tell you who could give you the scoop on him. That's a guy named Red. He got to know Parrot pretty well, and then the guy turns around and burns him." Jennings pushed aside a stack of papers on his desk. "I know that thing is in here somewhere. Isn't that the way things go? You can't find the thing you're looking for. But you got everything else in the world right there when you don't need it."

Trinity nodded. Watched Jennings sift through

the debris. If he could find Parrot's address, Trinity would be getting close.

Jennings pushed the pile of paper on the desk.

"Hey, at least I can give you the name of the casual labor place. They might be able to help you."

"How about Red? Does he still work for you?"

"Red only comes in now and again. He's basically retired."

"He would know how to get in touch with Parrot?"

"Oh, I should have said... Parrot's not his real name. I got his real name on his app if I could just find it."

"You don't have any idea where he lives?"

"No idea."

Trinity pulled out the picture of Lisa Brooks and handed it to Jennings. "Ever seen this girl with Parrot?"

"Nope. I never saw him with any girl. Like I said, the guy might been some kind of crazy. I wouldn't have trusted him around any girl." He took another look at the picture and then handed it back. "What's with her?"

"That's what I'm trying to find out. You got the name of the casual agency?"

"Just a second," Jennings said. "I know it's in here somewhere." He sifted through another heap of papers. "Parroti," he said.

"Parroti?"

"His real name," Jennings said. "Jerome Parroti, or something like that..."

"Anything else you can tell me?"

"He always talked about Indians. Like he had some friends living on the reservation. He said he was part Indian."

"He say which reservation?"

Jennings kept sifting through the pile.

Great, Trinity thought. This could be the end of the trail. How many reservations were there in Arizona? New Mexico? Trinity could see himself driving out some washed-out remains of a dirt road, looking for someone who somebody had heard might know something. The roads out there could be a challenge, even for the Bronco. Trinity didn't relish the prospect.

"Do you have Red's address?"

"Whoa, here it is!"

Jennings held the application up like a winning lottery ticket.

"That's great." Trinity tried to match Jennings enthusiasm.

"I got Red's in here somewhere too. Just hold on. Damn, I wish the wife were around. She'd pull it up just like that." Jennings snapped his fingers.

"Take your time. This is a big favor."

Jennings looked up.

"Happy to do it. I got a daughter too. She's older than yours is, but I wouldn't want her mixed up with nobody like Parroti."

There wasn't much information on Parrot's application. An uneven, loopy hand listed a reference from a casual agency and the unemployment office. No address. This was Trinity's lucky day?

"Wait," Jennings said. "Here's Red's."

Red's application was thorough. Using neat blue lettering, Red listed references, educational background, and his address.

Red was overqualified.

"A place for everything, and everything in its place," Jennings said, tapping the pile. "Lemme tell you one more thing. You find Parrot, you found yourself a sick one. I wouldn't trust him as far as I could throw him. Not after what he did to Red."

"What was that?"

"Hey, I've said enough. Let's leave it at that. Stole some stuff, I guess."

"What kind of stuff?"

Jennings shrugged. "I couldn't tell you. But I will tell you this. If your little girl's anywhere near Parrot, you need a gun."

WAITING FOR GAVINO

It pays to have a friend at the unemployment office, Trinity thought. Posters covered the sterile, welfare-green walls. Trinity waited for Gavino Ybarra to come out of his office. Trinity tried deciphering the languages on the posters.

Gavino shook Trinity's hand. Easily carrying three hundred pounds under his pink guayabera shirt, Gavino had probably doubled his weight since basic training in Fort Leonard Wood.

"Hey Frank," Gavino said. "This is great!"

He slapped Trinity on the back.

"How come you don't come around anymore? You need to come around, have a couple of beers, listen to some music. you know, just like the old times."

Gavino's face was round and expectant.

"Thanks, Gavino. I've been busy. You wouldn't believe it."

"Believe it?" Gavino looked around the office.

"I'm up to my ears here, myself… Hey Frank, so how long you been out?"

"Not long," Trinity said.

"Seems like yesterday, doesn't it?"

Trinity thought about it. It didn't seem like over twenty years since he first met Gavino. Both of them were heading to basic training together. Trinity from the university, Gavino straight out of the barrio.

Gavino had insisted Trinity meet his Tucson family after basic and maintained that they were adopting him as one of their own.

His face showed concern. "What's going on, Frank? What can I do for you?"

"You're a good guy, Gavino, aren't you? I didn't even have to ask."

"Hey Frank, you know me. Anything to help. What do you need?"

"What I need is a last known address. A phone number, whatever you got."

Gavino's face turned serious. "Who are you looking for?"

"It's a guy named Jerome Parroti. Last address unknown. Worked for a while at A-1 Exterminating. He was referred by a temp agency, prior to that he was seen by you folks. Maybe he was getting a check, maybe not. Supposedly the guy spent a lot of time on the street… Maybe a lot of time in the joint, too."

"Sounds like my kind of people," Gavino said. "Come on back and lets take a look at the fiche. I don't suppose you got a social?"

"Are you kidding me?"

"Just thought I'd ask."

"Actually, I do have one." Trinity had copied the number from the application. "Does that make it easier?"

Gavino laughed. "Are you kidding me?"

"Just thought I'd ask."

"Frank, you know you got to have a social just to take a leak these days."

"So it's come to that."

"Hey, it's the truth... What can I tell you." Gavino put on a heavy pair of horn rimmed glasses to look at the computer. His desk was government-issue gray with photographs of his family under the glass top.

Trinity glanced at the photos. "Everyone's gotten bigger since I saw them last."

"Yeah Frank. That's the way the world works."

Gavino paused in his search through a tray of microfiche. He pulled a thin piece of plastic from the tray.

"Like I say, Frank, you shouldn't make yourself such a stranger. Angie was just asking about you the other day. Her sister's still single, you know."

"The guy goes by the name of Parrot, if that helps any."

"The guy goes by the name of Parrot," Gavino mimicked. "The guy's name is Parroti and he goes by the name of Parrot. Frank, I've got to tell you, that comes as one hell of a big surprise."

"It shocked me too."

Gavino punched the social security number into the computer. "She likes you, too. I've got to tell you that. Angie's sister. She's a nice lady. You remember her, don't you?"

Gavino held his enormous hands in front of his chest. Scanned the long list.

"You should settle down. Okay, no place for nicknames on this thing. Just the facts, ma'am. You know, I wish we could put nicknames on these. It might make things easier."

He looked up from the screen.

"All right, give me that date-of-birth if you got it."

A new screen came up on the computer.

"That was easy," Gavino said. "Looks like we got your guy."

"Parrot?"

"Jerome Parroti. Went to the emergency room down at St. Rita's and they took eligibility information. It wasn't too long ago, either. Looks like it was a couple of weeks ago."

"Any idea what the visit was for?"

"Naah... Chronic dumb-ass, maybe? It feeds into our computer, so we got it. You wouldn't believe the stuff that comes up on this thing. Need the address?"

"That's what I'm here for."

"Coming right up," Gavino drummed his fingers against the glass top of the desk. "You're lucky you got it today. It could have been purged."

It was the second time Trinity had been told it was his lucky day.

"Why is that?"

"His address is in Oracle. That's Pinal County, not Pima. We've got our own indigents to take care of. You can have this."

He handed Trinity a printout.

"Thanks, Gavino."

Gavino laughed.

"I'll have Angie call her sister for you."

He held his hands even further from his chest.

"Talk about a lucky day!"

THE WATCHMAKER

A hedge of oleanders obscured Red's stucco house.

Trinity stepped out of the Bronco onto the gravel curb. A green plastic garbage can lay on its side spilling out sun-heated coffee grounds and half flattened beer cans. A sheet of black plastic peeked through the greenish-gray decorative pebbles in the yard, unable to hold back the invasion of weeds coming from beneath. On the concrete slab of a porch, a faded sofa and the remains of a washing machine were bookends on either side of the loose screen door.

Red was a big man, clean-shaved, his gray hair in need of a cut. He was bent over his kitchen table in concentration. A pair of magnifying glasses propped on his forehead, parts of several pocket watches lay disemboweled on the Formica surface in front of him. A short-sleeved western shirt hung loosely upon him as if the years had let him keep his size but robbed him of his power.

He barely looked up at Trinity.

"Door's open, come on in."

Trinity pulled on the screen door and stepped inside.

His eyes adjusted to the dim light.

A brown rag rug, slick with age, covered the hardwood floor.

Framed on the wall were two photographs.

In the first, a much younger Red rode a dazzling white stallion. The young man in the black and white picture was sure of himself, proud and confident as he faced the future.

The second picture was in color. Red held a baby in front of a rose-covered trellis.

Trinity introduced himself. Handed a card to Red, who looked at it through his heavy glasses.

"It's about Parrot, isn't it?"

"I'm looking for a girl named Lisa," Trinity said, "but yeah, Parrot too. They might be together. I thought you might be able to tell me where I can find him."

Red shook his head. "Parrot... He stole my car. Did you know that?"

"It's the first I've heard of it," Trinity said. "Did you report it?"

"I kept thinking he would bring it back."

There was a long silence in the room. Outside, a road crew jack-hammered the sidewalk.

"What kind of car?"

"Ford Fairlane. I've had it forever." Red smiled.

"Since before I moved in here. I bought it new."

"I think I've seen it."

Red took the magnifying glasses from his head and put them on the table. "Well, that's good news."

"Do you have any idea where Parrot lives?"

"Parrot could be anywhere. He's a drifter." Red paused. "Who's the the girl he's with?"

Trinity showed Red the picture of Lisa. "She's a sorority girl."

"Parrot would make a real splash at a sorority," he said, "unless they've changed since my day."

"Not that much. He may never have gone to the sorority. He was hanging around a frat. That's where I saw your car. That's where he would have met the girl."

"You think my car is still there?"

"That's where I saw it."

Red picked up a pen. "Tell me where it is. I'll go get it."

Trinity gave Red the address of the Omega House.

Red shook his head. "It's strange. Parrot and a sorority girl... How about some coffee?"

Red brought out two cups from the kitchen. "I take it you've never seen our friend?"

Trinity shook his head.

"Black coffee okay?"

"That's the way I like it."

"Parrot is a conman. Convincing as can be. He can make you believe anything."

"Did Parrot mention anything about an Indian reservation?"

Red snorted. "He rarely talked of anything else. It was just more of his little act. He was no more Indian than I am. Listen, I'm sorry, Trinity. I'm truly sorry I can't help you more."

He held the card Trinity had given him in his right hand and put on the glasses.

"Will you call me if you see him?"

Red nodded. He placed the card among the watch parts. "I'll do that," he said. "I'm very sorry about the girl, also."

It sounded to Trinity as if Red was offering condolences.

JOHN WAYNE

Ralph Jennings looked up at Edison and shook his head.

"You're the second one today asking about this asshole."

"Who else was asking?"

"A guy named Trinity. I've got his card around here someplace." Jennings pointed back at his overflowing desk. "He was a private investigator. But you..."

"I'm with the tribe," Edison said.

Edison had gotten from Holbrook to Tucson quickly. After the Salt River Canyon there had been practically no traffic from Globe all the way into Oracle.

Only when he got to the north end of Tucson had he needed to slow the F-150 down.

"I can't tell you anything more than I told the other guy. Maybe you should check with him."

"I'd like that, if you still have his card."

"Yeah, I got it. I stuck it on my desk."

Jennings went into the office and came back with Trinity's card and the applications.

"I forgot, I gave Trinity the old guy's address. The guy who worked with Parrot. Name's Red. He might be able to tell you something too."

Edison held up the application.

It was something, at least.

Something.

"I'm just going to copy these addresses," Edison said.

"Help yourself," Jennings said. "I sure as hell wouldn't want that greaseball Parrot messing with my daughter, either."

Jennings had a funny look on his face. "Hey, no offense, but I got to ask you something. Parrot made like he was an Indian. Was that the truth?"

Edison smiled at Jennings.

"Parrot's an Indian like I'm John Wayne."

SNAKE VENOM

Trinity drove the Bronco north on Miracle Mile until it turned into Oracle Road. The address was on the outskirts of Oracle and down a dirt road.

A stenciled plywood sign read SNAKE VENOM THIS WAY ONLY.

Trinity didn't think Parrot or anyone else would be out here. He pulled up next to a dilapidated aquamarine trailer. Dogs barked. There had to be twenty dogs in the trailer.

It was the end of the road. Gavino's read-out gave this as Parrot's last known address. The trailer was the only building on the place. Twenty dogs penned up in a tarpaper shack in the middle of a hot summer day outside Oracle, Arizona. Plus the possibility of venomous snakes

Trinity kept his door shut, gave the horn a blast and waited.

No answer. Another blast.

An old man peered out of a window, pulled the window open and poked his head out.

A flash of lighting crossed the sky, followed by a thunderclap. Where had this come from?

The sky turned black, then rain poured down in sheets. The lightning had to be close. The hairs on Trinity's forearms stood at attention. The washed-out gully of a road would soon turn into a river.

Stay too long, Trinity thought, and I'll be staying for the night.

The man yelled at Trinity. The rain was too loud for Trinity to hear his words. Another flash of lightning followed by thunder. The old man yelled, but through the window of the Bronco all Trinity could see were waving arms and a contorted face. He put the truck in gear and pulled alongside the trailer and lowered the window of the Bronco.

The man disappeared from the window before coming out of the trailer. He bounced up and down on the balls of his feet, screaming at Trinity.

"You're trespassing," the man shouted. "Turn your rig around and get out of here."

"I'm looking for Jerome Parroti. I've got a warrant."

"Never heard of him."

Aside from his rage, the man looked normal enough, even respectable. All the jumping around took a toll, though. He slumped against the door of the trailer, catching his breath.

Maybe there were more than twenty dogs in the place, Trinity thought. They sounded like the hounds of hell.

"Sorry to bother you," Trinity said. "I heard there was a man named Parroti living out here."

"Get out of the vehicle. Let me see you."

Trinity cracked the driver's side door open. Raindrops splattered down on the mud with the force of hailstones.

He proceeded carefully. The man could be more deadly than the snake venom advertised on the sign. Trinity believed in caution.

"Move slowly now. Don't you go and do anything sudden."

No movement crossed the man's eyes. He was blind.

"Keep your hands out in front of you," the man said. "No funny stuff now. You ain't got no warrant. You know I could shoot you right now and be within my rights. Ain't a jury in this state would find me guilty."

Not here. Not in this particular location, Trinity thought. The old man was probably right.

Trinity straightened to his full height. With one hand he held up the map of Tucson and with the other grabbed a screwdriver from his dashboard.

"Here's my warrant," he said. "While we're at it, I've got my badge, too."

The old man was still suspicious. "I guess if you're the law I got to talk to you. But I ain't got all day. What do you need?"

Trinity put the map and the screwdriver back on the dash. "I'm looking for a missing girl named Lisa Brooks."

No need to bring out the picture.

"She's with a guy named Parrot. You know

anything about him?"

"Never heard of her, but him I know. He's a worthless piece of trash."

Trinity waited.

It didn't take long.

"He did some squatting out behind that rise." The man pointed at the little hill behind the trailer. "Thought he was doing regular prospecting." The man paused. "Not that there's anything out there worth taking a look at."

His sightless eyes looked past Trinity as if to convince himself of Trinity's honesty.

"Soon as he got out there, I could tell he was nothing but a lousy four-flusher. Turns out he wasn't any kind of prospector at all. Had a hell of a wild party out there a couple of nights ago. It kept my dogs up."

"What day was that?"

The blind man scratched his face. "Couple days ago. I ain't heard a peep since then. But it sure as hell was wild that night."

"Mind if I cut through and take a look?"

"Long as it's all legal, you go ahead and take a look. But you ain't going to find nothing back there."

It depends on what you're looking for, Trinity thought.

He walked past the tarpaper shack. The dogs came to life again, snarling furiously.

BARLOW KNIFE

It was the landscape of another planet.

Boulders and saguaros stood against the mountain backdrop. The rain poured over the caliche, forming lakes in the wash.

Trinity walked along the wash until he came to a pile of empty beer cans. Maybe fifteen or twenty of them in a fire pit. It wasn't the scene of unchecked revelry that the blind man had described. He picked up one of the beer cans and smelled it.

They hadn't been there long.

The place smelled badly, even after the rain. It smelled like something dead and rotting.

The charred remnants of mesquite wood lay in the fire pit. The fire had gone out before all the wood had been consumed.

Maybe a sudden shower.

Trinity thought about the weather of the past couple of weeks. The monsoons had just started. Before that, unrelenting sunshine.

In the fire pit, Trinity saw the edge of something dull, flat, and gray. He kicked away the ashes with the toe of his boot and leaned over to pick up the small pocket knife that lay there, blade open.

Trinity remembered having a similar knife years ago. He had gotten it for Christmas wrapped in a small box with a penny taped to the lid for luck.

This one had the same brown, imitation bone handle with a little metal skirting, now rusted from exposure, with the word 'Barlow' engraved upon it.

He wiped the blade and handle of the knife with his bandanna and dropped it back into the pit, scuffing ashes over it with the side of his boot.

He stopped. He picked the knife up again, wiped it off, dropped it in his pocket.

There were tire tracks heading in all directions. Too many, Trinity thought, to make sense. There could have been any number of cars making trips back and forth.

Beer runs?

Or maybe something was being covered up.

Trinity took a few steps away from the fire ring. The smell made him gag.

The dogs howled.

He looked down and saw a man's corpse wedged between two rain-streaked boulders.

EXPOSURE

If anyone had looked, they would have found the man's remains immediately.

The foul odor was a giveaway, but Trinity hadn't been looking for a corpse.

Exposure bloated the body, and rain beat down on the purplish flesh wedged below Trinity. If the body still stank, Trinity thought, death had occurred only recently. The lab would give an exact time.

There was only the barest outline of a tattoo on the man's arm. To see it better required crawling down the rocks to where the body lay. The rocks were slick from the rain and the stench overpowered Trinity.

No way was Trinity climbing down there. It could prove impossible to climb back out.

A shabby tattooed dagger crept across the length of the man's arm with the inscription Fuckin' A.

No Parrot.

Trinity needed to report the body.

His boot tracks were all over the scene.

The idea of standing around waiting while local cops showed up and took his story didn't thrill Trinity, and his interchange with the blind man could lead to charges of impersonating an officer.

Nevertheless, Trinity climbed back up the rocks and got in the Bronco.

The dogs in the shack barked like sons of bitches.

CROWN VICTORIA

Deputy Sheriff Oscar Romo was drinking coffee in a pullout off the highway. The rain had started to come down again, beating hard against Romo's Crown Victoria. Trinity showed Romo his investigator's license.

Romo folded up his newspaper and snapped it against his thigh. "Damn," he said, "where did you say this happened?"

Trinity pointed back toward the exit. "Up there, past a couple of shacks."

"You're shitting me."

"You'd better follow me up there."

"Kind of wet going out there today, wasn't it?"

Trinity's shirt and jeans clung to his body, completely soaked and streaked with mud. Blood covered his hand where he'd scraped a rock.

"Yeah," he said, "I guess you could say that. It just started up when I got out there. Came out of nowhere. It didn't give me a chance to take cover."

The rain was really coming down now. Water

was filling the street.

A regular gully-washer.

It would have been a good day to stay home and watch the rain from his front porch. It would have been a better day for coffee at the Presidio Market.

Romo made a call and followed the Bronco up the dirt road and past the trailer. He got out of his car and the old man poked his head out. "Go on ahead, officer, look all you want. There ain't nothing up there, I'm telling you."

Trinity shrugged as Romo started up the trail. In the distance, a siren wailed.

Like Trinity, Oscar Romo wore boots with slick soles. Romo was having difficulty tackling the terrain.

"How much farther did you say that it was up there?"

An ambulance and another police car pulled into view.

"Not much," Trinity answered, "we should be getting to it."

The two men stood over the fissure looking down at the body.

There was no change, the face still contorted in a terrible stiff grin.

Only the strong smell of the man's body had made Trinity look into the crevice.

And luck had kept him from falling in.

His lucky day?

It was the stuff nightmares are made of.

The ambulance pulled up beside Romo's car.

"Are you going to need me?" Trinity asked.

"Only if you think this guy's going to get any deader." Romo was writing something. "I got your name. I'll let you know if we need you."

Heading down the trail was just as slippery. Trinity ended up sliding down part of the way.

This might be his lucky day, Trinity thought, but it wasn't getting him any closer to Lisa Brooks.

TRIBAL BUSINESS

He needed to take a shower and change into clean clothes before going back to the hospital. His white shirt was caked with mountain grime and the rain had soaked through his boots.

He needed to change everything.

And sleep wouldn't have hurt, either.

The man sitting in profile on the shadowy portion of Trinity's front porch was using a knife to carve a large piece of wood.

At Trinity's approach, he sheathed his knife and held the wood in front of himself for inspection.

Edison didn't stand when Trinity walked up the concrete steps.

"Trinity?" Edison said.

Trinity had never seen the man before.

He kept walking toward Edison, who put the wood down and dug into a briefcase at his feet. Trinity wondered what was in the briefcase.

He really needed the shower and change of clothes.

"Yeah, I'm Trinity. What can I do for you?"

"If you're Frank Trinity, you're looking for a guy."

Trinity looked at Edison.

The man looked straight-forward enough.

Strong.

An intelligent face.

"What guy?"

Edison looked steadily back at Trinity.

"A guy named Jerome Parroti," Edison said. "Also known as Parrot. You know where he is?"

"No idea," Trinity said.

Edison smiled and flipped the piece of wood over in his hands as if trying to make up his mind about something. Whether or not to show his hand. The piece of wood was smooth and somehow elegant. It also looked dangerous. The thing was big enough to bring down a deer.

Trinity stepped toward Edison.

"Why are you looking for him?"

Edison flipped the wood.

"We have a little business to conduct. It's got to do with the tribe."

As if that explained everything.

Trinity took out a business card from his front pocket and tapped it on the porch rail. The card was nearly as soaked as his shirt.

"Take this," he said. "You never know. Parrot's with a girl I'm looking for. You know anything about her?"

Edison took the card and stood up.

"That's news to me. I don't know anything

about a girl."

"I'm talking about a girl named Lisa. Nineteen or twenty. I have her picture in my truck."

He pointed at the Bronco.

Trinity didn't want to stay out here. He wanted to go inside. He wanted to take a shower and change his clothes.

"The chairman's not happy," Edison said. "I couldn't care less about the girl. You find Parrot, I'd appreciate you turning him over."

Trinity looked at the wood Edison held.

What was it supposed to be?

Edison paused. "I'll do the same for you though. If I find Parrot first, I'll make sure you get the girl."

Trinity stared at the wood. There was implied violence in the man's words.

Something told Trinity that Parrot didn't want to end up in this guy's hands.

Edison flipped the wood again. "Sound like a deal?"

Trinity looked at him.

"Maybe you should tell me how to get in touch with you."

Edison nodded. "Edison Graves," he said. "I'll write it down for you."

"You got a deal," Trinity said.

Edison ripped a sheet from his yellow pad and wrote his name and number on it. "Seriously, I gotta find this guy."

Trinity nodded. "You find him, call me."

He paused.

"What are you doing with that wood?"

Edison did a double take, then laughed. "It's going to be a flute. I'm working on it."

Edison stepped off the porch holding the wood in one hand and the briefcase in the other.

Trinity folded the piece of yellow paper and went inside.

ANTI-PSYCHOTICS

At the hospital, the nurse with the knitting bag had gone home and a man wearing long hair and a string of beads had taken her place. Trinity checked the nametag to make sure that the man worked there. Across the floor of the dayroom, Billy sat with his hands between his knees, shopping bag filled with clothing by his side, staring at an imaginary campfire.

"Billy's ready?" Trinity asked.

The man with the beads barely looked at Trinity.

"Yeah. And thanks for calling, by the way. We were kind of sweating it out to see if anyone was going to pick him up." He looked at Trinity. "I've gone over Billy's med schedule with him. The anti-psychotics are really important."

"You can say that again," Trinity said.

"The lab reports show that Billy ingested about twenty times the usual amount of mescaline we're used to seeing."

"The usual amount?"

"Every now and again we get someone here who's been on peyote. It's not that frequent, and they can only take so much at a time. They usually throw up most of it."

"Billy didn't?"

"Mr. Carton, your son was distilling pure mescaline from the peyote buttons. Gradually it seeped into the pores of his skin. He had no idea how much he had taken."

"Billy's always been clever."

"That's why it's so important that Billy stays out of the toxic environment that he's been living in."

The man leaned toward Trinity.

"He needs to change his playgrounds and playmates."

Trinity gave a fatherly grin.

"I couldn't agree with you more," he said.

"We've contacted a few places. I think we'll be able to get him in some kind of residential treatment facility, if you think that's appropriate."

Trinity squinted at the man's nametag.

"Bruce," the man said.

"Of course, Bruce."

Trinity pushed out his hand, not wanting to press his luck.

"You guy's have been terrific," he said. "More than terrific."

Bruce beamed.

"Let us know how things are going. We're

always here for you."

Across the room, Billy looked up from the shopping bag. Trinity walked up and put his hand on Billy's shoulder.

"Billy," Trinity whispered, "Bruce over there thinks I'm your father. Do us all a favor and save the crazy act at least until you're out of here."

Billy looked at Trinity.

"Right, Dad," he said.

LONE RANGER MEETS THE FATAL BELLMAN

Edison drove the red pickup north on Campbell Avenue. How much did this Trinity know? Edison wanted to get away from the dense city center and think things over.

The steep foothills of the Catalina Mountains marked the end of Campbell. Just past Ina Road, Edison pulled the truck over and parked it in the shade of a mesquite. He dug into the plastic bag next to him and pulled out a piece of jerky. He chewed on the strong meat and took a swig of water from his flannel covered canteen.

Edison smelled the creosote which always followed Tucson rain. Two crows played in the updraft from the mountain face. Edison followed their flight. Icarus. Was Icarus the father and Daedalus the son? Edison couldn't remember. He knew the father fashioned the wings for the son. And then the son flew too high.

Edison shrugged. It was Edison who left the reservation. Edison who got the education. And yet what did he really have to show for it all? He picked up the stick of cottonwood and tapped it against the dashboard of the F-150.

Most people had looked down on Livingston. But what would Livingston have done with the opportunities Edison enjoyed?

Edison shuddered.

When Edison heard him in the truck, Livingston's voice had been clear.

"Show me some respect, Little Brother."

He could easily have gone to the cops and told them what Duane said. He didn't need to be in Tucson chasing his brother's killer like the Lone Ranger.

And if it came to killing, would he be equal to the task? Edison wasn't at all sure of that.

Livingston's whole life, from the rodeo arena to his last days at the Sunset Motel had been a long flirtation with death. It made Edison sad that death came to his older brother in such a sordid way.

But could he take another man's life in vengeance? Edison wasn't sure he wanted to step onto that bridge, much less cross it.

One of the crows flew away and the remaining one drifted down and landed on a stump in front of the F-150. The bird shook out its shiny black wings and hopped around almost facing Edison.

Edison chewed the jerky and looked at the bird. Crows were supposed to live to a vast old age and he had heard that they were among the most intelligent of birds.

He wondered how fast they traveled.

Could this crow have followed Edison from the reservation?

His professors would have called them harbingers of death, citing Poe's raven or Lady Macbeth's fatal bellman. But that wasn't quite right, Edison thought. Edison's thoughts were bleary from fatigue. An owl symbolized the bellman. But it could easily have been a crow.

Edison knew in the instant of the crow's flight what he would do. It wouldn't come down to killing. But Parrot might wish it had.

CALL ME FRANK

"You're going to drink that?"

Billy sat at Trinity's kitchen table, watching him stir a mixture of honey and orange juice.

"No," Trinity said, "you're drinking it. It's good. You're lucky, I was thinking about sauerkraut and carrot juice. Compared to that, this stuff is a walk in the park."

Billy gagged. "I don't want it."

"Drink the whole thing, Billy. It's good for you. All your nerves are shot and the dope they gave you just postpones the inevitable."

"What do you mean?" Billy stared at the glass. "When are we going to find Lisa? Isn't that what we're doing?"

"Drink this and shut up for a while. Give your brain a chance to breathe."

"My brain's breathing? How can my brain be breathing." Billy jumped up. "I'm sorry, I've got to go. I've got a really important appointment. What did you say you're name was?"

Like the White Rabbit, Trinity thought.

He's late.

"Trinity."

"Oh yeah, right... Trinity. You're right. It's Trinity."

"You can call me Frank," Trinity added.

"Hey, that's great, Trinity," Billy said, "but listen, I really do have an appointment and I have to be going."

"Sit down, Billy. You don't have any appointments. You just got out of the hospital." Trinity pointed at Billy's blue plastic wristband. "You want me to cut that thing off?"

"Oh yeah," Billy said. He exhaled heavily. "Definitely. Hey, You're going to help me find Lisa, aren't you?"

"That's right, Billy. You've got it right on the money... You hungry?"

"I guess so," Billy said.

"Think you could manage a cheeseburger?"

Trinity grabbed the keys to the Bronco.

AVOIDING THE TOXIC ENVIRONMENT

While Trinity steered the Bronco onto Kino Boulevard, Billy opened the paper wrapper and stared at the Whataburger.

"Where are we going?"

"Your father." He headed the Bronco toward Sixth. "I can't take you back to the frat. I think your friend Bruce would call that a toxic environment. We have to avoid that."

"Don't worry, I'm not taking any more of that stuff." It sounded like a message written on a blackboard. "I've learned my lesson."

"That stuff in your room at the frat. Does it belongs to you?"

"No."

"Who does it belong to?"

"I don't want to talk about it."

"Where's Lisa, Billy. And don't try to con me."

"If I knew where she was, I'd tell you. I'd go get her myself."

"You would?"

"Yeah, I'd get her." Billy straightened his shoulders, pleased with the idea.

"So you got no idea where she is now?"

"I already told you to ask Parrot."

"I thought you were trying to wise-ass me."

"Not about that... I'm serious. Parrot would know."

Billy's eyes went blank again.

"Billy," Trinity said, "This Parrot. He's an old guy, right?"

Billy turned with a worried look. "You know Parrot?"

"I've heard of him."

"He's bad."

"Did he live at the frat?"

"No, he just showed up one day. He lived out in the bushes in some cardboard boxes."

"When was this?"

"This spring. He just came in off the highway or something. Said he'd gotten skin poisoning from the sun in El Paso."

"Why do you say he's bad?"

"He is... He wasn't the kind of guy you could trust, you know what I mean?"

"Yeah, I do," Trinity said. "You say he lived in the bushes?"

Billy nodded.

"And he had a parrot tattooed on his arm,

right?"

"Yeah, a big one." Billy spread a hand over his own forearm to show the size.

"What else can you tell me about him?"

"He thought he was God's gift…"

"Lady's man?"

Billy snorted. "Yeah, what a joke."

"What else?"

"Like you said, he was old. He tried to act younger but I'll bet he was at least thirty-four or thirty-five. Maybe even older. I couldn't tell you. Maybe even your age."

Billy gave an apologetic look.

"His face was messed up. Like worse than just a bad sunburn. He always walked around with his shirt off like he had this great body."

"Why did you guys let him stick around?"

"It wasn't like he was living there. He was just out back under the bushes. I guess at first nobody noticed."

"When was the last time you saw him?"

"I don't know. Everything's kind of fuzzy still."

"I imagine it would be."

Trinity slowed the car.

Billy looked out the window.

"Hey," he said. "What is this place?"

"It's your father's house, Billy. I'll check on you the first thing in the morning."

Trinity watched Billy walk toward the house, holding his shopping bag and the small paper bag containing his medications. He stopped in front of

Mr. Carton's front door.

A light came on and then the door opened.

Trinity couldn't see the father, but Billy went into the house.

A CALL FROM THE EMERGENCY ROOM

Lesley met Trinity at the door of the Presidio Market.

"You need to call the hospital, Frank."

"What's going on?"

"I wrote the guy's name down… " Lesley looked concerned. "Dr. Evans at the Emergency Room. St. Rita's. He said something about your card."

Trinity put his arm around her waist and kissed her.

"Sorry Lesley, I've got to go. I'll call you."

"Be careful, Frank."

EYES OF A DRAGON

Trinity caught nothing but green lights on Speedway heading west toward the hospital.

Billy was safe. As safe as he could be inside his own skin.

Turning south, the signs in the shop windows changed to Spanish. Trinity steered the Bronco past a Day-Glo red low-rider cruising slowly in the direction of the setting sun. Trinity rolled his window down to take advantage of the evening breeze.

An illuminated white cross shone above the hospital roof. Slamming his brakes, Trinity wedged the Bronco into a parking spot near the emergency room door, almost hitting a Plymouth Fury as he threw open his door.

The electronic doors of the hospital let out a blast of air conditioning. The admitting clerk didn't bother to look up from her novel.

"Help you?" she asked.

"I need to talk to Dr. Evans. I got a call from him."

"Have a seat. I'll see if he has a minute." The clerk motioned across the expanse of linoleum tiled floor toward a row of burnt orange space-age chairs. A cart loaded with mops, sponges, and disinfectants propped open the door of the men's room. It was too early for the knifings and gunshot victims that punctuated most Saturday nights.

The only other person in the waiting room was a man wearing a sleeveless fatigue shirt and a pair of rubber sandals. The man had loose tobacco spread out on a People magazine and was talking to himself while rolling a cigarette.

The clerk disappeared into the treatment area.

Trinity walked over to the ambulance bay. The lights of the city twinkled like the eyes of a dragon in a darkened tunnel. The man in the fatigue shirt twisted up the magazine and shook the remaining tobacco back into a pouch.

"You're Frank Trinity?"

The doctor was younger than Trinity expected. Standing in scrubs, he held out his hand to Trinity.

"We found your card. It was in the pocket of a boy who was brought in a while ago. It was all he had on him. We hoped you could identify him."

Trinity and the clerk followed the doctor into the treatment area. Two nurses stood chatting while an intern wrote in a chart. At the third bed the doctor pulled the curtain aside.

Mark lay on his back hooked up to an

intravenous needle. His eyes were black and blue slits, his face swollen like a bruised grapefruit. He was not awake.

"How bad is he?"

"Not nearly as bad as he looks. But he got dumped here. Nothing in his pockets for ID except your card. Do you know him?"

Trinity looked at Mark. He barely recognize him as the boy from the Omega House. Someone had beaten him badly. Left him nearly dead.

"I talked to him a couple of times at the fraternity house where he lives. Gave him my card, obviously."

"You know his name? He won't be able to talk for a while. We've got him knocked out.

"Then what?"

"Then what do you think?" The doctor patted Mark's shoulder. "We send him home with a serious suggestion that he stay out of fights."

"His first name is Mark. I don't know his last name. You don't know who brought him in?"

"Like I say, he was dumped here. Happens all the time. He nodded toward the admitting clerk, who clearly would have liked to get back to her reading. "You can ask Bobbie about that.

Trinity would be willing to bet that Bobbie was too preoccupied with her reading to notice particulars about Mark's arrival. Trinity might as well have asked Bobbie about Saturn's rings.

"I heard the car, but I can't see the outside area from where I sit. This place gets busy, too."

"I'll bet it gets busier as the night goes on."

"You know it."

The waiting room was still nearly deserted as Trinity walked out of the ER and toward the exit.

❋ ❋ ❋

"I been here all night. They still ain't seen me."

It was the man in the fatigue shirt.

Trinity walked over to the man who perched on the edge of one of the bolted down chairs. "Did you see the car that dropped off that boy?"

"I been here damn near all night. What the hell do you think?"

The man gave a disparaging look toward Bobbie who returned it with a scowl of her own. The man's face was deeply pitted and a bulbous nose spread out over it like an over-ripened tomato.

"Tell you the truth," he said, "I could use a cup of coffee."

There's no such thing as a free lunch, Trinity thought, but sometimes there's coffee.

There were vending machines in the corner of the room and a couple of tables. Trinity brought two cardboard cups to the table filled with black coffee. The cups showed a five-card hand of poker. Empty, the cups could be turned over to show a draw card.

The man was in no hurry to give Trinity the information that he wanted.

"Much appreciated," he said, first blowing

across the top of the cup and then taking a sip. "Black. How'd you know that's the way I like my coffee?"

"Wild guess," Trinity said.

"Well that's the way I like it, partner. A good cup of joe."

Actually, Trinity thought, the coffee was pretty weak, even for vending machine coffee. He was going to need a second wind pretty soon and the coffee wasn't going to provide it. Trinity let the man ramble.

"Like I said, they ain't even going to look at me. I could be dying out here and do you think they'd care?"

Trinity assumed the question was rhetorical.

"If I came in here dying do you think they'd do one thing for me?"

"Are you dying?"

"Hell no, I ain't dying. I'm just asking. But if I was, they wouldn't do nothing for me. I may not be dying but that don't mean they got any right to treat me like I ain't even here. I been here all night and they won't even talk to me. All they say is that my eligibility is up. Which is a lie."

The man stabbed the Formica table with a blackened fingernail to emphasize his point.

"You a social worker?"

"No," Trinity answered.

"Well, I thought you could be. You look like one. Every time I come in here I get the runaround."

"You saw the boy get dropped off here?"

"I seen it all, brother."

The man assumed an attitude of authority. He tapped his hand against the left pocket of his fatigue shirt.

"Damn," he said, "I was sure I had some smokes left. You ain't got no smoke, do you bro?"

Trinity shook his head.

"That store over there." The man pointed at an all night convenience store down the street. "That store got smokes. Lucky Strikes'll be fine, bro. LSMFT, right? Lucky Strikes means fine tobacco."

He broke into a grin exposing two rows of rotted teeth.

"Can't smoke in here though. That's the rules."

"You saw the person who dropped off the boy?"

The man gave a sage nod. "I told you I seen it all, bro. That store over there? They sell wine too. I wouldn't mind a little old bottle of muscadoodle."

It only took a few minutes.

The clerk at the convenience store rang up Trinity's purchase. A bottle of muscatel wine and two packs of Lucky Strikes.

Might as well live it up, Trinity thought. It was a night on the town.

"That's it for tonight?" The clerk's moustache was halfway between cop and walrus. Headphones hung around his thick neck.

Trinity watched himself in the grainy screen on the video monitor mounted in back of the clerk. He couldn't tell if he looked more like a gunfighter or a social worker. Maybe a combination of the two.

Counselor with a gun.

"Yeah," Trinity said, "I guess that'll do it." He considered saying that the stuff wasn't for himself.

Why bother, he decided.

"Hey," he said, you didn't notice some people bringing a kid in to the hospital earlier, did you?"

The clerk didn't change expressions. "I just got on. Besides, you can't keep track of what's going on over there. You need a bag for that?"

"Yeah, and a receipt."

Brooks could payroll this party.

The man was standing by the electric door when Trinity returned. He snatched the bag from Trinity.

Trinity was glad to help the guy. It was fine with Trinity. Next year he might give a little less to the United Way.

Skip the middleman.

"JR's the name, bro. Pleased to make your acquaintance." He held his hand out for Trinity.

Another soul handshake.

Just like Mark gave him. A couple of real hepcats.

"What kind of car was it?"

"What car's that?"

"The car that dropped the boy off. The one I was asking you about."

"Oh, that car."

JR scratched his gray hair. He held a stiff ponytail in place with three dirty rubber bands. He was working hard to dredge up the recent memory. The car hadn't pulled up any more than a couple of hours previously.

Trinity supposed that JR was trying to distinguish the car from all the other that had pulled up to the ER that night. It would take a while to wait for JR's synapses to snap into place.

"Yeah, JR said, "I saw the car."

He fell silent, scrutinizing one of the packs of cigarettes.

The silence exasperated Trinity, but it was like fishing. You have to give the fish some line.

Trinity didn't like fishing.

"Good," he said. "Would you say it was an old car or a new one?"

JR dug his hand into his jeans pocket, extracting. a wadded book of paper matches. He stubbed the first match against the striker.

Pfft.

The match was a dud.

Same for the next. JR was going to go through the whole book. Trinity pulled out his Zippo and snapped it open for JR.

JR wasn't in a hurry. He tapped the first pack of Lucky's first on one side of the pack and then on the the other end. He rolled the pack on its side and tapped the edges.

"Damn tobacco companies are so scared of lawsuits, they don't roll these things like they used to. They don't put as much tobacco in. Plus they make more on each pack," JR said. He cupped his hands around the flame. "A lot more."

There was no wind. The cupping of the hands was a habitual jailbird reflex. JR took a drag on the filterless cigarette, held the smoke in deeply and finally exhaled. The yellow-orange light of the ambulance bay coming in through the door caught the smoke and held it in a pattern above JR's head.

"That's a good smoke," he said, "I been smoking these for a long time."

He shook the pack toward Trinity.

"Want one?"

Trinity shook his head.

"You remember the car?"

JR looked surprised. Jolted out of a reverie.

"The car? It was a blue Fairlane. Had one just like it at one time. A damn fine car."

"Who was in it?"

"It was an old guy. Pretty strong though. Just lifted that kid out like he was a baby."

"Tell me what he looked like."

"I would if I could, bro. Tell you the truth, I didn't see him that close. But you could tell that car anywhere."

JR was enjoying his moment in the spotlight.

"Are you a cop?"

"No," Trinity said. "Not a cop, not a social worker."

"You kind of look like a social worker," JR mused. "No offense."

"None taken."

Trinity looked back into the waiting room. Two nurses were chatting about a bridal shower.

They were healthy and good-looking. Alive in the middle of a sterile death-like interior. In the neon lighting of the room, nothing was hidden. Trinity watched the nurses for a moment. Betty on the right. Veronica on the left.

PRESIDIO AFTER HOURS

A few things can be figured out while driving late at night and Trinity soon exhausted these.

Mark and Billy were both injured and neither were likely to provide useful information any time soon.

Trinity felt guilty about Mark's beating. Whoever was running the dope lab up in Billy's room must have figured that Mark was responsible for kicking in the door. If that were the case, they must have beaten him up thinking he was about to become a snitch or a rip-off. Whatever the cause, it was a brutal beating. Trinity's sick hunch was that Mark might not have any more information to give to him.

On the other hand, Mark must have known about the contents of the room. He had brought Trinity there, after all.

It was too small a house for anything like a drug lab to go unnoticed. The stench would have alerted anyone in the vicinity to the unusual science project being constructed on the premises.

The Bronco practically steered itself to the Presidio Market. The evening was over and the store was closed. Lesley sat at a glass top table, totaling the day's receipts. Seeing Trinity, she unlocked the front door to let him in.

She smiled at him. "Have you eaten? I could make you a sandwich or something."

She wore a denim skirt and sleeveless blouse. A pair of kicked off sandals lay beneath the glass table.

It had been hours since he had eaten. He told her about Mark's condition.

"Where was he going?"

"I told him to call me here. He didn't get a chance. He had my card in his pocket. That's why the ER called me."

"What happened to him?"

"I think whoever was working the lab up in Billy's room came back and flipped out. Mark isn't the fastest of talkers. They saw the place had been broken into and figured he'd been in there. Put two and two together and came up with five. They nearly left him for dead."

"Are you sure it wasn't the other boy's stuff? The boyfriend's. What's his name?"

"Billy? No, I don't think the stuff was Billy's. I mean, he said it wasn't his."

Lesley looked at him.

Trinity also had his doubts. Billy was out of his

tree. And Bruce at the hospital had said the peyote buttons had been distilled. That would explain the green mash. But if the stuff belonged to Billy, why had Mark gotten beaten up?

"You look tired," Lesley said.

"It's been a long day," he said. "Extra long."

"Who took him to the hospital?"

"I wish I knew. It wouldn't have been the same guy who beat him up." Trinity's fatigue caused things to swim around him, but he knew the answer.

"A guy at the hospital said it was an old man... Sounded like the same car I saw at the frat house."

"An old guy in a car you've already seen. Shouldn't take too long for you to figure this thing out, Frank. Any other description?"

"Who needs more?"

A few minutes passed without either speaking.

"You should go home," Leslie said. "You fell asleep. Are you okay to drive?"

"I'm fine," he said.

Thinking about Lesley kept Trinity awake for the few blocks he needed to drive. The thoughts postponed Trinity's bleary descent into sleep and pushed recent events from his mind.

SHOWER AND COFFEE

Trinity woke late. Fully clothed on the couch of his living room.

Outside, the street was quiet and a shaft of light came through the window dancing against the waxed surface of the hardwood floor.

He started a pot of coffee in the percolator.

A shower cleared his head.

Back in the kitchen, he poured a cup of coffee and sat down.

Strong coffee.

A good cup of joe.

He knew who took Mark to the hospital and where to find the car.

RED'S HOUSE

The Bronco felt like a blast furnace. Trinity kept the door open for a minute before sliding into the drivers seat.

The door to Red's house was open. Trinity pushed aside the screen, walked inside and yelled for Red.

No answer.

The watch pieces were still spread out over the table and Red's magnifying glasses were perched in a case next to a half-filled cup of coffee. Trinity felt the side of the cup.

Stone cold.

Trinity took a closer look at the pictures on the wall. Red's history could be traced from them.

The picture with the horse was from back east, somewhere. There was grass in the background and trees.

The second picture, the one of Red and the baby in front of the roses had probably been taken in Tucson. The corner of a tile roof peeked into the picture.

In the second picture Red looked prosperous

and healthy.

The epitome of fatherly pride. Something had changed in Red's life.

Something caused him to move away from the comfortable domestic life he'd enjoyed into this shabby bungalow.

Where he was now sprawled on the linoleum tile of the kitchen floor.

The contusion over his eye probably was inflicted by a fall. A nearly empty bottle of vodka stood on the kitchen counter. He breathed heavily through his mouth.

Trinity shook Red. The older man groaned and Trinity stopped. The cut above the eye was bad. It was purple and open. He would need stitches. Trinity shook him again.

Red's eye cracked open and focused unsteadily on Trinity. "I got my damn car back. It's out back. Take a look."

He closed his eyes again. There was no point in trying to awaken him again.

The Fairlane Trinity had seen at the Omega House was now parked in the overgrown weeds of Red's backyard. Probably the same one JR saw at the emergency room. Red went to the Omega House and found Mark beaten and near death. If Red was the Good Samaritan who took him to the hospital, he had probably saved Mark's life.

Trinity went back into Red's living room. He took a card from his pocket and wrote a note on the back for Red to call him. He left it by the magnifying glasses.

The big man began to move.

Trinity shook Red again.

"What happened to you, Red?"

"Son-of-a-bitch," Red moaned. "That son-of-a-bitch Parrot cold-cocked me when I got back here. He wanted to take the damn car again… Borrow it."

"Why didn't he just take it?"

"I barely got it home. It was on it's last legs. Damn thing doesn't work anymore, that's why."

THIRD-PAGE STORY

Trinity bought a copy of the *Arizona Daily Star* on the way back from Red's. A story on the third page told about the discovery of the dead man. Trinity's name appeared deep into the write-up as a local detective who found the body.

The body was that of a drifter named Albert Church. Police said indications pointed to a recent time of death.

So far, according to the article there were no known suspects or motives for the murder.

The newspaper's main story was about the heat.

Tucsonans were being reminded to use less water on their lawns, and to avoid prolonged exposure to the sun.

CREDENTIALS IN ORDER

Two men stood on the porch, waiting for Trinity's return.

"Ray Farmer, Pinal County," the first man said. He held out a badge. A shock of white hair, barely too long for a crew-cut.

Trinity looked at the badge.

Farmer nodded toward the other man. Much younger. Korean features. "My partner. Harvey Park."

Trinity's mind was on Red. He wondered if he should have taken Red to the hospital. He really looked like he was in bad shape.

"This is about Oracle, right?"

Farmer scowled. He wore loud green slacks. The kind worn for golf or St. Patrick's Day.

"You won't mind telling us what you're working on, right?" Farmer brushed off the front of his pants. "I take it you weren't just messing around out there for your health, were you?"

"I'm looking for a girl. She's off with some

character named Parrot."

Trinity looked from Farmer to Park.

"That name ring any bells?"

Farmer wasn't listening.

"I understand. That's just fine. You were army CID, right?"

Trinity nodded.

"That's good, very good. Marine Corps, myself, but you got the credentials. Lot of guys think they can open up shop after a couple of years on the force. Hell, you don't know a damn thing until about ten years."

Farmer stopped. Looked at Trinity.

"Did you know the guy you found out there had been stabbed?"

That surprised Trinity. He had assumed the fall had killed the man. The newspaper hadn't mentioned a stabbing.

"Knife wound in the the left armpit. You wouldn't have seen it unless you were sticking your fingers in there or something." Farmer grinned. "Course, couldn't fool the coroner. I watched it myself. Me and Park, here."

Park looked disinterested in Farmer's story.

"We got the body identified as Albert Church. No known address. What a mess. You think your deal is tied in with this?"

Trinity shook his head.

Park spoke. "You got a make on the guy you're looking for?"

"Parrot?"

"Yeah," Park said. "Has he got any kind of record? Have you checked?"

The question exasperated Farmer. "Whattya think, Park? This guy is CID."

Trinity interrupted. "I haven't checked."

Turning toward Park, Farmer rolled his eyes. "Well, hell then..."

Farmer turned back to Trinity. "Harvey, I believe we got a little problem here."

FLASHLIGHT ON THE STAIRCASE

The dark night arrived before Trinity got back to the Omega house. The air after the afternoon downpour still smelled of creosote. He parked next to a hedge of oleanders and walked half a block up the street to the fraternity.

The door to the darkened building was open. Trinity whistled softly and walked in. Turning a flashlight on the the staircase he could see only shadows. No light or sound came from the upstairs hallway.

Billy's room was locked. Trinity crawled out of a hallway window and onto the tile roof.

The night air was cool after the rain. He crouched next to the stucco wall. The stars were out and the moon was a sliver. Students walked past the house and from his perch Trinity heard snatches of conversations.

"You are?" a tall boy with curly hair walked with a slim dark-haired girl.

"You're right," the girl said. "She's absolutely the

worst."

"But that's only if you're looking at it through western eyes."

The voices grew distant and started to blur. Trinity tried warding off sleep, but found himself drifting off and quickly jerked his head up.

He awoke.

Checked the luminous face of his Seiko 5.

His nap had lasted at least forty minutes and he'd been in a crouching position the entire time.

He heard voices from inside the house.

Instinctively, Trinity hugged the building more tightly. A poster covered most of the window and Trinity could only peek through a crack at the bottom into Billy's room. A dark figure holding a duffel cleaned out the room like a cat burglar. Nothing incriminating was being left. Trinity tried to quietly wedge the window open.

A rock would have worked better. The window wouldn't budge.

As quietly as possible, Trinity slid down the tiles of the roof. He dropped from the roof between the house and the oleander bushes. A pile of cardboard boxes broke his fall.

He pulled the Bronco alongside the house and waited with his lights off. The dark figure came out of the house, lugging the duffel bag. Trinity recognized the baggy shorts.

Mark had gotten out of the hospital.

SAFE AS MILK

In the bright lights of the late-night coffee shop, Mark's face was still puffy with stitches under both eyes. He was telling Trinity he had returned for the dope because it was valuable.

"You got any idea what it's worth?"

"I wouldn't know," Trinity said. "How are you planning to spend it when you're dead?"

"Come on," Mark said, palms flat on the table. "It's there for the taking."

Trinity had heard variations of that line before. Usually from men heading for long periods of incarceration.

"Who beat you up, Mark?"

Mark looked into his cup of coffee. He added another packet of sugar and stirred. It was the third packet. He reached for a non-dairy creamer.

"Maybe I don't remember."

"And maybe you're dumber than I thought. Was it a guy named Parrot?"

"So what if it was? I got his stuff now."

"How did you get to the hospital?"

"Can't remember."

"Ever met an old man named Red?"

"Never heard of him."

"You're coming with me."

Trinity wasn't sure what else to do with the kid, and he could use whatever information Mark could give him.

"Lose the sack."

The last thing Trinity wanted to do was carry dope in the Bronco. Things were hard enough to explain. He pointed at the oleanders.

"Just dump it in the bushes over there."

"You think it'll be safe?" Mark looked concerned.

"Safe as milk," Trinity said. "You'll be safer without it, that's for sure." Trinity looked at Mark. "Now I want you to think for a minute. You've got an assignment here. You're going to tell me where we can find Parrot."

"Man," Mark said, "you can't find Parrot. He could be anywhere."

"Tell me about it."

"I mean it. How am I supposed to know where he is? You think Lisa is with him?"

"Could be. Start talking."

"I don't know."

"Cut the bullshit. Start talking."

"There's supposed to be a party tonight," Mark said.

He held his hand up to the stitches over his eye.

"Off Fifth Street. Parrot could be there."

ANOTHER DEAD-END BLONDE

Trinity overshot the party and parked about a half of a block away.

"Is this the place?"

Mark nodded.

"You stick around with me," Trinity said. "If this doesn't pan out, I'll want some other ideas. Start thinking about that."

Mark didn't look happy.

"Hey," Trinity said, "maybe we should have a little chat with the narcotics officers downtown. I'm sure they would be fascinated by the contents of that bag. I'm on pretty good terms with those guys. You think they'll believe your story or mine?"

Mark looked miserable.

"No funny stuff in this place, Don Juan," Trinity said. "You go in there, and if you see Parrot, you tell me right now. Is that clear?"

Mark nodded.

Trinity realized there was no reason to trust

him.

He waited while Mark went into the house. Too much time passed. Leaving the Bronco, he walked down the alley behind the house. Hedges and a slump block wall separated Trinity from the party.

Nothing to it.

He scaled the wall and watched from the bushes. Flames danced from a fire in the back yard. Strings of Italian lights hung from branches of a palo verde tree.

A boy and girl lay entwined on the ground away from a small fire, close enough for Trinity to see and hear them.

A police helicopter circled above the party and trained a spotlight on the backyard. Trinity caught a glimpse of the girl's face.

Another dead-end blonde.

Not Lisa.

Trinity wedged through the crowd near the keg and walked into the house. His reflection in a hallway mirror caught him off guard, as though he were seeing someone else.

A tall girl with curly red hair rubbed the front of Trinity's shirt. She had a purple crescent moon tattooed on the back of her hand.

"Hey," the girl said, "I couldn't find you."

"Hey," Trinity said.

The girl stroked his chest. Beads of perspiration showed on her upper lip.

"Hey," Trinity repeated.

The girl stopped. She backed away from him,

giggled. "Oh, it's not you."

"No problem," Trinity said. "That's what I was trying to tell you."

"Sorry," she said, "I thought you were…"

Trinity stepped away. "It's all right. Maybe your friend's out back."

No sign of Mark in the house.

In the alley, the passenger side of the Bronco was open.

Mark was gone.

ON THE QT

The lights on the answering machine were flashing when Trinity woke up. He remembered ignoring them the night before.

He made coffee, took a shower, then hit the button to listen to the message while drying.

Edward Brooks was irate. He wondered if Trinity was the man for the job.

Find someone else, Trinity thought. Or do the job yourself.

Someone knocked on Trinity's door.

He grabbed a freshly starched shirt from his closet and headed toward the door.

Another knock.

"Cool it," he said, "I'm getting there."

Ray Farmer's assistant, Harvey Park stood on the front porch. He looked over his shoulder as if to make sure nobody was listening.

"Coffee?" Trinity said.

Park shook his head. "I'm strictly here on the QT. I got some information about your man."

Trinity motioned toward the porch rocker and Park sat down and put his briefcase in his lap.

"You know that you can't..."

Trinity interrupted him.

"You don't have to worry about me. I haven't seen you."

The file Park pulled from the briefcase had been obtained from a friend who worked at the prison in Florence.

"You work fast," Trinity said.

Park nodded.

"This is definitely a bad actor you're dealing with. You want to do whatever you can to get that girl away from him."

The document described Jerome Parroti as a sociopath. In and out of foster homes since he was a boy. Juvenile detention in Michigan, Missouri, and finally Arizona.

Charges ranging from shoplifting to aggravated assault with a deadly weapon.

He had used heroin, inhalants, amphetamines, and prescription barbiturates, starting out with alcohol at age nine.

Trinity tapped the paper. What about glue-sniffing?

Parroti did not feel he was addicted to any substances. He had been released after a seven year stretch in Florence six months before. The seven years represented eighty-five percent of a term for aggravated assault. The details of that crime were particularly brutal and the judge had commented while sentencing about Parroti's apparent lack of remorse. Notes also indicated that the prognosis for rehabilitation was not hopeful and that his sentence had been imposed prior to the commencement of much harsher mandatory sentencing.

Blah blah blah...

The report meant that if he screwed up again, Parroti would be well into geezerhood before seeing the bright lights of the outside world.

Parroti reported to community supervision and currently held a job in telephone sales.

Trinity gave the report back to Park.

"The telemarketing gig is a thing of the past."

Park made a note.

"I'm not kidding. Don't tell Farmer or anyone else I gave you this stuff. He's old school. Kind of touchy about that kind of thing."

"No problem," Trinity said, "if there's anything else I can do for you, let me know. Same goes for your partner."

Park laughed.

"You know, Ray is a really good guy. I've learned a lot from him."

"I can tell," Trinity said.

Park got into his white Caprice.

No doubt about it, Trinity thought, that couldn't be anything but a cop car.

He turned back toward the door. A clatter came from the alley and he saw Elmore come out from behind a trash can.

It's Ali Baba, Trinity thought.

Elmore was wearing the same grimy purple

pants and the leather vest, but today he wore a flowered turban that looked a little like a pillowcase. Under the vest he wore a sleeveless MIT sweatshirt.

"Trinity my man," Elmore said, pointing at the receding Caprice, "since when do you hang out with *Adam 12*?"

Trinity laughed.

"Occupational hazard, I guess. How long you been there, Elmore?"

Elmore shrugged.

"I thought you got all that Joe Friday out of your system. Start making friends like that, you gonna lose the common touch."

"I appreciate your concern, Elmore. What brings you down here?"

The walk from Fourth Avenue to the Presidio, especially in the heat of the day was a real hike.

Elmore smiled, shook his head and held the palm of his hand up to Trinity.

"First things first, my man. My throat seems to be parched unto dryness."

Trinity went to his front door.

"I'll make you some ice tea."

"Very generous, Trinity."

Elmore took the stub of a yellow joint from the lower pocket of his pants and rolled it between his thumb and forefinger.

"A glass of tea would be appreciated. I particularly enjoy the raspberry herbal variety."

"I got Lipton's. You see any more of that Parrot

guy?"

Elmore smiled.

"Maybe. Since you ask so nice, might as well tell you all about it."

Trinity came back toward Elmore.

"What you got?"

Elmore looked amused.

"How about that tea, first?"

Trinity pulled out his wallet and extracted a ten.

"How about you tell me what you know first, Elmore?"

Elmore shrugged.

"If you insist. Trinity you need to know that you ain't the only one looking for Parrot. There's a big Indian dude asking every freak on the street if they know Parrot. I don't think he's the man, but a lot of people not as sure as me."

Elmore gave Trinity a look.

"You know this dude?"

"I met him," Trinity said. "His name's Edison."

Elmore nodded.

"Like the light bulb."

Trinity looked at Elmore.

"Do you know where Parrot is?"

Elmore rolled the yellow joint between his fingers.

"That's what I'm here for," he said. "Let's just say, I run into a dude that knows Parrot, knows him well enough to be able to follow him and see where he goes."

Elmore held the joint under his nose, inhaling deeply as he spun the construct.

"Let's say this friend of mine been hearing Parrot offering to sell certain Native American hallucinogenics. Might explain the interest of a certain Indian named Edison. Could be that Edison is the peyote police."

"This guy knows where Parrot is?"

"Let's say he does. It might take a while, but we could line this up. We'll just have to see. See if he shows up again. But I'd need some bus fare. I ain't making this walk again."

Trinity smiled.

"Did you cut the same deal with Edison?"

Elmore laughed.

"Tell you what, Trinity, since you and me go back so far, I'll give you thirty Mississippis for a head start."

THE TRUTH ABOUT ORACLE

Billy stood in front of his father's house when Trinity arrived. There was no sign of Mr. Carton. Billy's eyes glimmered in recognition.

"Billy, you need to tell me the truth."

"The truth?"

Billy made it sound like Trinity was speaking Sanskrit.

"Do you know where Lisa is?"

"No."

"What happened in Oracle?"

A shadow fell between Trinity and Billy. The boy was silent.

"Something happened there, didn't it?"

Billy nodded.

"Something."

"You need to tell me. Whatever it was."

Billy loooked up at Trinity. Tears had formed in his eyes.

"It was dumb. It shouldn't have happened."

"Keep going."

Billy started to fall apart.

"It was an accident. We were stoned. Totally stoned. Tripping on the peyote buttons. You wouldn't even know what that's like. Lisa was the one who wanted to go there. I never liked Parrot. I couldn't stand him, you know? But she thought it would be this great thing."

He stood for a while. Not saying a word.

Trinity watched him.

Finally, Billy continued.

"I didn't want to be out there. I was scared. Now, if something's happened to Lisa, it's my fault."

"Mark took off with the stuff in your room. Was he out there with you?"

"No, it was just me and Lisa. And Parrot. The other guy showed up after we started tripping."

Billy tried to cover the tears spilling down his cheeks.

"Other guy? You knew the other guy?"

"Sort of. I mean I'd seen him with Parrot. It's hard to remember exactly what happened."

Trinity nodded.

"He just came up to the fire while we were sitting there. He started going after Lisa, like he was going to rape her. Parrot put the knife in my hand, but I swear I didn't do anything to the guy. I couldn't have. I gave the knife back."

Billy was shaking.

"What did Parrot do then?"

"He made a big show like he was going after the

guy with the knife he took from me. But he didn't. It was just a pocketknife. Just a little pocketknife. He dropped it into the fire."

"Then what?"

"Then he went after the guy with a different knife. A real knife. The one he wears on his belt. For real..."

"What happened then, Billy?"

"Parrot must have stabbed the guy. The other guy ran away from him. He didn't get far before he fell. He must have snapped his neck or something. It was bad. I never saw a dead body before."

"What did Lisa do when all this was going on?"

"Lisa was freaking out. She was out of her mind. We'd taken the buttons and she was tripping... Screaming... Out of her mind. Then..."

Billy's face went blank.

"Then?"

"Then Parrot grabbed her. I tried to help her but he had the knife. He was pointing at me and telling me to get out of there. There was blood on his knife. He said he could prove I'd killed the guy. I didn't know what to do. He said that if I told anyone about this, he would kill me. He was crazy..."

Billy looked up at Trinity with clear eyes.

"He is crazy. You're the only one I've told this to."

"You left Lisa with Parrot?"

"It's worse than that."

How much worse could it get? Billy would be

punishing himself for the rest of his life.

"Worse?"

"I can't even say it. She told me... She told me to get lost. She wanted to stay with Parrot."

"What did you do then?"

"I started walking. I'd come down a little, I guess. I walked away from there. Before I got to the car I guess I wanted to do something, so I threw a rock at him as I was leaving. I was hoping I'd hit him. But the last thing I saw they were still by the fire."

"Together?"

Billy shrugged.

"I guess Lisa really thought he was cool. That's why she wanted to go out there with him. I should have said something, but she wouldn't have listened."

"How long have you known Lisa."

"Just a few months. We weren't really going together. I wanted to, but she wasn't interested in me that way."

"Did she know Parrot before this?"

"She'd never seen him. He'd been hanging around the frat house. I went along with the act when I saw him with the buttons. But she went for the whole routine. I just went along for the hell of it."

"She drove?"

"No, I drove. That's how I got back. I drove my own car."

"I thought you had eaten the peyote."

"I didn't say I did a good job of it. I finally just left my car. I kind of got distracted and started walking. I thought the stars were talking to me. I walked the rest of the way. The car probably ended up getting towed."

"That's how you ended up in the hospital?"

"I still hadn't come down. There was something else I didn't tell you."

"What's that?"

"Parrot had all those buttons in his backpack?"

"Right."

"So he threw the backpack in the back seat of that car he was driving around. I took the backpack."

"You took them back to the frat house?"

"Right. That's when things got messed up."

More messed up, Trinity thought.

"So the last you saw of Lisa, she was with Parrot?"

"What was I going to do? I thought the guy was going to kill me. And she didn't want me around. She..."

"Do you want to stay here?"

Billy looked at his father's house. He nodded.

SOME WEAPON

Trinity knew two more things. Edison was looking for Parrot like a bull picks out a china pattern.

He also knew that the dead man wasn't just an unidentified corpse. The corpse had a name. Albert Church. Parrot had killed Church. Parrot somehow convinced Lisa to stay with him. She told Billy to get lost, even though she had just seen a man knifed to death. Parrot got Lisa to start asking her father for cash. Still, the equation didn't quite add up.

Who introduced Lisa to Parrot? Billy said Lisa had never seen Parrot before that night. Why did she want to stay with him? Billy's story had some credibility at least. If Lisa had seen Parrot before, she might not have wanted to stay with him.

Trinity still had the knife he had found in the fire pit. It was in his pocket. The same one Billy described, the Barlow knife with the brown handle. There were a million of the things floating around. He pulled out the short folding blade. Some weapon.

THE PONY

"Daddy, I need some money."

It was the first time Trinity heard Lisa's voice. She sounded like a little girl.

Brooks stood next to the tape recorder like an expectant father.

He had skipped any chit-chat with Trinity. He wanted him to hear the recording.

"I really need the money. It's got to be ten thousand, Daddy. Please? That's not even as much as you paid for my pony."

Lisa could have been asking for the keys to a car. Or permission to stay overnight at a friend's house.

"Trinity, that's a hell of a lot of money my daughter's asking for."

Trinity nodded.

"You're putting it in her account?"

"I already did."

"How much does that make?"

"Enough."

Brooks face was ashen.

"Trinity, that's not the significant part of her

call."

"What do you mean?"

"When Lisa was little, she always wanted a pony. She thought she could keep it right here at the house."

Brooks looked like he had been stabbed.

"Trinity," he said. "I never bought Lisa a pony."

SEAT BELTS

Trinity wondered if Mark went back to the Omega House after the party.

It was worth a look.

When he saw Trinity, Mark ran. The alley in back of the Italian restaurant was short. It was a Dumpster and a dead end.

Trinity grabbed Mark by his shirt and belt and pushed him back toward the car.

"Come on," he said, "we're taking another ride."

Mark tried to pull out of Trinity's grasp.

"Where do you think you're taking me?"

"To get the truth out of you."

Trinity pushed Mark into the Bronco and slammed the door shut.

"No seatbelts?"

Mark dug his hand under the front seat.

"Don't worry about it," Trinity said. "You don't need them. We're just taking a short ride. Try to think clearly."

Trinity accelerated the Bronco over the trolley tracks.

Mark's head hit the roof of the truck.

"Comfortable?"

"What are you doing?" Mark screamed.

Trinity hit the gas again. A gully. The truck caught air.

"Think about Lisa. I want you to concentrate."

Trinity leaned on the wheel and the truck swerved west onto University Boulevard.

"You need to give me something to go on. What do you know?"

"I don't know anything about her. Haven't you talked to Billy?"

"Billy doesn't know anything. I'm betting you do, though. Am I right?"

"I can't tell you anything."

Mark pushed himself deeper into the front seat.

Trinity gunned the engine toward the desert.

"I'm not kidding," Mark said, "don't you have seatbelts?"

"I forgot," Trinity said. "You're from the seatbelt generation."

Mark pushed his hands further down into the crack of the seat.

"Take your time," Trinity said. "Free associate."

The Bronco's speedometer edged toward ninety.

"*Albondigas* or *menudo*? Betty or Veronica? Just say the first thing that comes into your mind."

Mark reached behind the seat.

"Are you crazy?"

Trinity rocked the Bronco back and forth on the open road.

Mark's body slapped against the door.

"Hey Mark," Trinity said, "I wouldn't count on finding the seat belts. Oh, and sometimes? The door over there pops open for no reason."

Mark clutched at his seat.

Trinity hit the brakes.

Mark's body slammed against the glove compartment.

"Brakes work great, though."

Trinity backed the Bronco up and revved the engine.

Mark tried to climb into the back seat.

Trinity grabbed his shirt with his right hand and pulled Mark back.

Trinity hit the accelerator and swerved toward the side of the road, coming within a foot of the guardrail.

Mark slammed against the door again.

"I told you that door doesn't stay shut," Trinity yelled. "Sometimes it just flies open."

Mark screamed.

"Come on, kid," Trinity said. "Live it up. What do you know about Lisa's roommate?"

"Wendy?"

"That's the one."

"Slow down and I'll tell you."

"Say the magic word."

"Shit," Mark said. "What are you, fucking nuts? Please slow down."

"That's more like it."

Trinity slammed the brakes again.

Mark flew into the dash.

He dragged himself back up onto the seat.

Trinity looked at Mark's face.

They did quality work at St. Rita's. The stitches were holding up nicely.

Trinity slowed the Bronco.

"Why don't you tell me a little about Wendy."

"She's out of my league."

"Did you talk to her?"

"I did. A couple of days ago."

"She tell you anything?"

"Yeah, she said her life wouldn't be complete until you jump her bones."

"Seriously?" Mark looked at Trinity.

"She didn't tell me anything. She said she was late for work."

Trucks and cars whistled past the Bronco.

"What else do you know about her? Any reason she'd be lying?"

"I don't know. She didn't hang around the frat."

Mark stared out the window.

"I think she and Lisa had a fight."

"When was this?"

"It was nothing. I heard Wendy say she missed going up to Lisa's house to do laundry. That pissed Lisa off for some reason."

"Why would that piss her off?"

"You tell me," Mark said. "Lisa's like that. Touchy."

Trinity pulled the car off the road. His imagination was developing a half-formed picture.

"Ever meet a guy named Albert Church?"

"Who's that?" Mark asked.

"Ever been up to Oracle?"

Mark gave a blank look.

"Not sure where that is."

He didn't know anything more.

They were about five miles from the frat house.

Trinity decided to give him a ride back.

Exposure to the sun wouldn't do Mark a bit of good.

CRACKED CONCRETE

After Trinity dropped Mark at the frat house, he pulled back onto the now-thick afternoon Speedway traffic. He parked in front of Wendy's house, walked up the cracked sidewalk, and knocked on the door.

A woman in a white terry cloth robe opened the door.

"Wendy's not here. I'm Gwen," she said.

In hoop earrings and high heels, she looked like an older version of Wendy.

"She won't be home until later," Gwen said.

She pushed a lock of hair from her eyes.

"Do you two have a date?"

The light from the overhead fixture made the room look even more barren than it had the other day.

"I need to ask her a couple of questions about Lisa Brooks."

"I can't tell you when she'll be back."

Gwen's voice was seductive.

"Why don't you come in? I'll put something in the blender. You like margaritas?"

Her white robe opened slightly.

"Wendy's friends are my friends too."

Trinity didn't move away from her. Judging from her breath, the blender had already been put to use.

"Maybe some other time," he said. "I need to find her."

Gwen put her hand against his chest.

"It's that important?"

"Life or death."

"What has my little girl gotten herself into this time?"

Trinity waited.

This was Wendy's mother.

She lifted her head to put her lips next to his ear.

"You can find her after eight," she whispered. "Do you know a place on Fourth Avenue called the Kashmir?"

TWO MORE MESSAGES

There were two more messages on the machine.

Edward Brooks was upset.

He wanted a status report, ASAP.

The second message was more interesting.

Pamela Chambers voice breathed from the machine. "Frank Trinity?" she said. "I hope you remember me." She paused. "I'd like to talk to you again. I think I can help."

Trinity felt his pulse quicken.

He remembered Pamela.

He tapped the button on the machine.

No more messages.

Almost eight o'clock.

Time to surprise Wendy at the Kashmir.

BELLY DANCING

At the Kashmir, a woman in a snakeskin sheath danced on a small stage. A sitar played on speakers while she rubbed her hips. Smoke and a veil obscured much of the dancer's face. Trinity watched as the woman worked her hands from her hips to her waist. A small diamond gleamed above her navel, sparkling against her skin's almond tan.

Wendy stood in the back of the club. Recognizing Trinity she gave him a fingertip wave.

He followed her to a small table at the back of the club.

"I'm sorry," she said, "I forgot about our little conversation."

An amused expression crossed her face.

"You were asking me about Lisa?"

She nodded toward the stage,

"I've got a little time before I get ready for my set."

"You dance?"

She let a cigarette dangle from her fingers.

"I'm the best."

Trinity pushed a book of matches toward her.

"Do I tip you now or after you go on?"

On stage, the dancer held a candle in each hand, flames unaffected by the undulation of her hips.

"Did you find Lisa yet?"

"I've barely started looking for her."

Wendy's eyes betrayed nothing.

"Why are you here?"

Trinity looked at the stage.

"I like culture."

She looked at him again. Angrily, this time.

"I mean it. What do you want?"

"I understand you went with Lisa to the Omega House. Is that true?"

She took a deep drag on the cigarette.

"What difference does that make?"

"Did you?"

"God, what a dump. Yeah, I've been there a couple of times. Not my style."

"You know most of the guys there?"

"Most of them?" She put the cigarette out. "I wouldn't say that. Maybe a select few."

"Anybody named Parrot?"

"Oh sure, he was there."

She looked disgusted.

"What kind of place lets somebody like that hang around? I told Lisa he was a reject."

"But Lisa liked him?"

Wendy laughed.

"You could say that. Lisa is very naive. She thought he was some kind of genius. She…"

"Go on…"

"She thought he was a victim of society. She actually said that. So stupid."

"He's violent, Wendy. He almost beat a guy to death. And then he did the same thing to another guy, the man who took the first guy to the hospital."

Wendy looked up.

"When did this happen?"

"It just happened. You think she's still with him?"

"I'm positive of it. Is Edward worried?"

"You know Lisa's father?"

"Edward and I are close. He told me that Lisa still blames him for breaking up with her mother."

"Sounds like you've talked with him a lot."

"He's a sweetheart. He's not perfect. But then, who is? He's been lonely ever since Lisa left home to live in the sorority. She's five miles away, but it might as well be a thousand."

"Brooks says she brings friends up to swim and do laundry."

"That's true."

"Do you have sex with him?"

The question amused Wendy.

"Do I screw him? Is that what you're asking me?"

"Yeah, that's what I'm asking."

"We're friendly. Very friendly. Ed is very warm and a very talented man. To tell you the truth, I was attracted to him, and I'm sure he would have been willing. But Lisa was always there."

Trinity nodded.
"I suppose that would be awkward."
"You could say that," she said.
She stood up.
"Time for my set. Stay if you like."

A MINOR LEAGUE CURVEBALL

Edward Brooks was irate. He stormed around his living room.

"Trinity, correct me if I'm wrong. I'm paying you good money to find my daughter. And you come up with what?"

He paced in front of his paintings. They were impressive. As Wendy said, Brooks had talent. Trinity wondered if any of the talent remained.

"You're paying me, Brooks, but you didn't tell me the whole story. I had to get that from Wendy."

"My God," Brooks said. "What did she tell you? Never mind, don't believe anything she says. She's a pathological liar."

"All right, enough of the name-calling. What's she got on you?"

"Nothing… Nothing really happened. Though God knows… She paraded around here like…" The incomplete simile hung in the air like a minor league curve ball.

"Knock off the puritan act, Brooks. I've seen her and talked to her and I don't buy it. You liked it."

Brooks put his face in his hands.

"Lisa walked in on us. I don't suppose you know what that feels like?"

"Probably embarrassing. But I'm just guessing."

Trinity looked out at the pool.

"Brooks, your daughter is what, nineteen years old? She must have had some idea what you and her friend were doing."

Brooks went to the bar for another drink. He squinted with bloodshot eyes, measuring two shots into a tumbler.

"I don't feel any guilt, Trinity. Not about Wendy. I just feel badly that Lisa found out about us that way. Wendy is very mature for her age. Lisa is not."

"How old is Wendy?"

Brooks sat on the edge of the couch and took a sip from his drink.

"I couldn't tell you."

Trinity left him. What difference did it make how old Wendy was? It didn't make any difference. But it bothered Trinity. Bothered him like a persistent itch. If Wendy was any less than ten years older than Lisa, Trinity would need proof. It was late. Too late to call Lesley. Too late, he thought, pulling the Bronco into his driveway. Too late, he thought, staring at the phone. There was something wrong. Something missing. He knew where to start.

In the morning.

WATER LILIES

Pamela Chambers said she would be at the sorority house all morning. Her anthropology seminar didn't meet on Mondays.

After a quick call to Meredith at the administration building, Trinity drove to the house.

She welcomed him at the door wearing a white skirt and a light yellow top. She had on the same squash blossom necklace.

Trinity liked the outfit. It was subtle, and the squash blossom lent an anthropological appeal.

She held her hand behind her head.

"Sorry I was so rude the other day. I thought about calling you to apologize."

"You apologized before I left here. Look, I need your help."

"What can I do?"

"Do you keep the records for this house?"

"What kind of records?"

"Addresses, birthdays, that kind of thing."

"You need Lisa's?"

"Not Lisa's, Wendy's."

"Well that's easy enough. Come with me, detective."

Like the living room, the study was decorated in pastels and white leather. Yearly pictures of the sorority members lined the walls along with Monet's water lilies. Trinity glanced at the composite photographs while Pamela leaned over to open the bottom drawer of a file cabinet.

"Chandler. Wendy Chandler. It says here that she's a legacy. That's news to me."

Pamela smoothed the pleat of her skirt as she stood up.

"Her mother, I guess. That would mean she would almost be an automatic bid."

"Anything else?"

"Just the usual. What did you want to find out?"

Trinity stood in front of Pamela.

"How well do you know Wendy?"

Pamela shook her head.

"Truthfully, not well at all."

"Any reason she wouldn't be on the composite?"

"What are you saying? She should be there."

"Take a look. She's not on it."

There was no Wendy Chandler on the composite.

"You have a student directory here?"

"Somewhere, I suppose."

"No need to find it. I'll tell you what it says. There's no record of anyone named Wendy Chandler taking classes this year either in the fall or the spring."

Meredith had only taken a minute to confirm that information.

Pamela looked embarrassed.

"I should have been more careful, I guess?"

Trinity shrugged.

"What seemed unusual about her was her age. I didn't believe she was just out of high school."

Pamela moved closer to Trinity.

"I just can't believe this. Usually the house is so close-knit."

She was very close. Close enough for Trinity to smell her perfume. It was a familiar scent."

"Look," Trinity said, "it's not the first time something like this has happened."

"Trinity," she said, looking into his eyes, "I know this is a funny time to say this, but I really would like to see you again."

He could feel her breath on his neck as she twined her hands behind his head.

"Mondays are normally free?"

He put his hand on her waist.

"All day," she said.

She slipped onto the white leather chaise. The movement was sudden enough to draw the midriff of her top upwards. A sudden peak, quickly covered, but long enough.

The diamond flashing from below her navel was no surprise.

Trinity had seen it before.

"You're a hell of a dancer, Pamela. Sorry I didn't leave a tip."

The Kashmir. It was a nice sideline these girls had.

Pamela pushed herself up from the chaise quickly.

"What's that supposed to mean?"

"Save it, Pamela," he said. "I liked your act. Still do, as a matter of fact."

"What's wrong with making some money?"

"Absolutely nothing," he said. "I just need you to tell me where Lisa is."

Her eyes narrowed.

"You have to leave now."

Trinity walked toward the door.

"Keep my card," he said.

ROLL OF NICKELS

Red's stucco house needed more than paint. Whole hunks of plaster lay on the ground exposing the adobe walls. Trinity didn't bother knocking.

Wendy was attending Red, who lay on a couch, nursing a can of Schlitz. His bandaged head made him look like a war casualty.

Wendy barely looked up at Trinity.

Trinity hated to disturb them.

"Doing better, Red?"

"I suppose. I got kicked by a mule. That sure as hell wasn't his fist, I can tell you that. The little coward had to be carrying a roll of nickels."

Wendy stood up. "What are you doing here?"

"It's all right," Red said. "I know this guy."

"How about you, Wendy? What are you doing here?"

"I came to help my father. You said he'd been hurt."

Red was confused. He looked from Trinity to Wendy.

"You know him too, Wendy?"

"He's a friend of a friend," she said.

Red looked at her. "A good friend to have."

"I need to see you, Wendy," Trinity said.

Standing outside the house in the slight shade provided by the stoop, Wendy threw her head back, barely looking at Red.

"Tell me where they are," Trinity said.

"Even if I knew, I wouldn't tell you."

She arched her back against the wall of the house.

"Parrot would kill me. I mean that literally."

"You wouldn't be the first."

Trinity stopped. Wendy was frightened.

"I also mean that literally."

She pulled out a cigarette. No elaborate lighting ritual this time. She pulled a book of matches from the cellophane.

Trinity gazed away from the house toward the mountains. Heat emanating from the asphalt created small waves in his vision. A scorcher.

"He might do it anyway," he said. "Kill you, I mean. Just for fun. How did you hook up with him, anyway?"

Broad daylight had stripped any mystery from Wendy. What remained was pure fear.

"Oh my God," she said, "you don't think that I actually..."

"No, of course not. I don't think he's your style."

"I met him here. My father was trying to help him. Parrot was like a project for him. Red's not perfect."

"But who is?" Trinity broke in.

"Exactly," she said. "Who the hell is?"

"Why did you join the sorority in the first place?"

"My mother was a member. Back in the good old days. I couldn't believe they accepted me. I'm probably the last person who would join one. But I liked it. That's why I stayed."

"How did Parrot meet Lisa?"

"I shouldn't have done it, but I put the two of them together."

"Why would you do that?"

Her eyes narrowed.

"I wanted to get back at her. Edward loves her. I never would have a chance with him with her on the scene."

It was as simple as that. She said it plainly, and Trinity believed her.

"She couldn't stand the fact that you were her father's lover?"

"Exactly. We were in bed when she walked in. She freaked out. It didn't make any difference to her that I'm older. Anything I said made it worse. She was screaming. You would think someone had been killed. Then she said she wanted to kill me."

They stopped talking. Red had come outside and was walking slowly toward them.

"You gotta admit, Trinity, she's a hell of a girl."

Trinity nodded.

Red wasn't lying.

"Course Gwen raised her."

Trinity looked at Wendy. A lot had happened since Red had held her next to the roses. A little girl always grows up.

"I met Gwen."

In the sunlight, Red looked healthier than when Trinity had seen him hunched over his watches. He was standing upright in the Arizona sun and Trinity could see a radiance around the man he hadn't noticed before.

"You met Gwen too?"

A smile crossed his face.

"Well then you saw she's a hell of a woman, too. Damn stupid of me to let her go."

REAL LIFE ANTHROPOLOGY

Red and purple clouds streaked the sky over the mountains as the sun went down. On his front porch, Trinity slumped on the rocker. Parrot could be halfway to hell for all anyone knew. Trinity's eyes closed and he drifted toward sleep.

Halfway to hell. Would he need to go there?

No. The trip could be a waste of time.

And dangerous for Lisa.

❊ ❊ ❊

The sky was dark when Trinity woke up.

The phone was ringing.

"Trinity?" Wendy sounded panicked. "You work with a guy named Edison? He told me that you two work together."

"I work alone, Wendy."

"I thought so. I didn't know whether to talk to

him. But I know something else about him. I know about him and Pamela."

So that was it. Pamela and Edison. The bachelor and the bobby-soxer. The Indian and the sorority girl. Girl anthropologist comes from Pennsylvania out to the Wild West and meets a living specimen of Native culture.

Trinity put his hand to his forehead.

"Pamela's in trouble, Trinity."

"Why?"

"Do you know why her boyfriend is looking for Parrot?"

"He told me it had something to do with the tribe."

There was silence.

"That was bullshit, Trinity."

Wendy's voice was all business.

"Edison told me Parrot killed his brother."

"Edison's brother?"

Trinity's mind reeled. What was this all about?

He thought about Edison flipping the stick in the air. A flute, he had said.

"That's right," Wendy said. "His brother up on the reservation. Parrot killed him. Edison's brother's name was Livingston."

"Wendy," Trinity said, "where does Pamela live?"

THE MISSING LINK

The apartment shared by Edison and Pamela was in a white-washed slump block complex on 1st Street.

Wendy had provided the missing link.

He hoped he wasn't too late. He didn't expect to see Edison at the apartment. By now he would be at least one step ahead of Trinity.

Trinity opened the unlocked door.

Pamela Chambers, sorority advisor, belly dancer, anthropologist, lay on the floor, partially hidden by a sheet. Beaten, not sleeping. Trinity had guessed correctly about the primordial urges, anyway.

Belly dancing...

Peyote...

Enough raw material for more than one dissertation.

Trinity knelt over her prostrate body.

Felt for a pulse.

RAW MATERIAL

She was still breathing. Thank God for that, Trinity thought.

"Where are they?" Trinity said.

Pamela groaned.

She turned her head and he saw her neck. The squash blossom necklace was gone. Replaced by a bruise crossing her throat and working its way across her face.

Trinity led her to the Bronco and gently helped her into the front seat.

"Why did he do it?"

Pamela winced. "He thought that I..."

Trinity waited. It could take a while for her to answer.

"He thinks I'm responsible... For Livingston getting killed. I'm not, you know."

Trinity headed once more toward the emergency room.

At the bay, he turned toward Pamela.

"I'm leaving you here."

She nodded.

"You know where they are, don't you?"

She turned away from Trinity.

"You've known all along. And when you wouldn't tell Edison, he beat you to get you to tell him."

"No," she said, "it wasn't like that."

She was a complicated person. What else was she besides the various personas she had adopted? Edison had figured it out. Pamela had sent Parrot up to the reservation. She wanted to try the peyote herself. Why? Was it curiosity? Raw material for anthropology graduate seminars? Did she plan to become the female Carlos Castaneda?

Something in her eyes told Trinity it was more than any of those things. Something which he couldn't explain. He'd seen the look before, but he hadn't expected to see it on Pamela. But there it was on her face. The bleeding and bruising made it doubly worse.

It was a look of sickness. A soul sickness Trinity wouldn't have imagined. How many people had been affected?

Brooks. Lisa. Wendy. Edison. Billy.

Two men were dead.

Maybe Parrot had tried to buy the peyote and things had gone wrong. Maybe he had just planned to use the knife to prepare the buttons.

Pamela started to shake.

It had been one act after another.

The sorority act. The anthropology act. The Kashmir.

If Edison could be this violent, Pamela was

lucky to be alive.

Trinity put his hand under her chin.

"I would have passed the blindfold test, Pamela," he said. "I can tell when you are lying."

She shook her head. Her eyes would be black and blue for a while and then they would return to whatever was normal for her.

"You set it all up, didn't you?"

"No, no, no…"

She buried her face in her hands.

Trinity pulled her head up and forced it close to his own.

"You set it up. You sent Parrot up to the rez. Tell me now or tell the cops."

She shook her head again.

"Tell the cops after there's been another murder."

He turned her face toward his own. Her eyes were streaked and swollen now.

"How many murders will this make? Three? Four?"

He pushed her back toward the seat.

"I guess you would only be an accessory to three. You might get less than twenty."

"All right," she said. "What do you want?"

MOTEL MESCALITO

Trinity pulled up to the abandoned motel. The moon lit the ragged stucco exterior and near the empty office, the remains of a neon sign stood as a darkened sentinel. Chain link and concertina wire surrounded the property.

The fence was far from impregnable.

Trinity had breached fences far more challenging.

Pamela's directions had been accurate.

She had known Edison for a semester before they moved in together. Pamela met Edison's brother Livingston in Holbrook when Edison took her there. She felt like she was becoming one of the family.

Edison had given her the squash blossom necklace. It had belonged to his mother.

She had listened to Livingston's stories. He told her about flying with falcons over the canyons.

Meeting with spirit warriors.

Speaking with animals.

Who wouldn't want those experiences?

The way Livingston related them brought them to life.

Made them real.

She imagined what the experience would be like.

And then she asked Livingston if she could try the buttons.

Take the peyote.

Livingston was shocked.

He had said no.

Never.

But Pamela couldn't get the idea out of her mind. In Tucson, Wendy had told Pamela about Parrot, whom she had met through her father. Pamela talked to Parrot. Asked him to do her a favor. Parrot agreed to do it. She hadn't expected the result.

Not in a million years.

Trinity looked at the fence.

He had scaled taller ones in a matter of seconds.

And he could break into the room's window in even less time.

Parrot had been only too willing to make a little trip.

In previous years, the motel had been a Tucson landmark, but now there was no sign of life in the place.

A darkened neon sign still stood with a woman diver eternally caught in mid-plunge over an advertisement for ice-cold refrigeration and a pool.

No sign of life now except Edison's truck parked near the street.

Trinity looked into the motel window. He could see Parrot and Lisa and hoped they couldn't see him yet.

Parrot reached for Lisa's arm in the darkness of the motel room, fiercely pulling her to her feet.

Edison had to be around here.

Trinity looked over his shoulder.

No Edison.

Parrot was smaller than Trinity had expected. No more than five foot six, Trinity guessed.

The parrot tattoo looked like amateur's work.

He was holding a dark brown backpack.

The same backpack Mark had thrown in the bushes by the fraternity.

Lisa didn't look like her pictures. Her hair was close-cropped and bleached almost white.

Trinity pulled out his gun and waited.

Lisa let out a scream when Parrot grabbed for her hair, and unable to hold it, slapped her across her face.

Using her arm as a fulcrum, Parrot slung Lisa toward the door of the room and still holding the backpack, pushed her forward.

Still holding his gun, Trinity took out a bandanna, and wound it around his fist.

He wouldn't be able to wait long.

"Listen, you little bitch..." Parrot hissed the

words, stumbling forward as he approached her.

Lisa cringed, bracing herself for Parrot's fist.

Parrot's ankle hit the corner of the bed and he wailed.

Lisa drew her breath in quickly and put her hands to her mouth.

Trinity also inhaled, still watching.

Not time yet.

Parrot looked up, dropped the bag and limped slowly toward Lisa, rubbing his fist into the palm of his hand.

"Might as well give you something to remember me by."

Glancing at Lisa, Parrot pulled a switchblade from his jeans pocket.

"Jesus, no," she said.

Softly, like a prayer.

Parrot laughed.

He flipped the blade out and held the knife overhand. He didn't notice the small crack of light that played across Lisa's face.

A shadowy figure of a man holding a wooden club opened the door and stood behind Parrot.

Edison wrapped the club around Parrot's throat, then grabbed his arm and brought the switchblade down swiftly, burying the razor-sharp blade deep inside Parrot's upper thigh.

Parrot opened his mouth, gasped, let out a soundless scream.

Soundless at first.

Trinity counted.

One, two, three.

He smashed the plate glass with his fist and jumped into the room, training the gun on Edison's head.

Parrot howled.

Edison grabbed Lisa in a headlock and pushed her toward Trinity.

She stumbled, falling on the ground at Trinity's feet.

"Go ahead, man," Edison said. "She's all yours."

Trinity kneeled on the dirty floor next to Lisa.

She looked up at him with the barest glimmer of comprehension in her eyes.

"It's okay," Trinity said. "It's okay, Lisa. You're safe."

His eyes were becoming accustomed to the dark.

Edison shook a few of the peyote buttons out of the bag. They were wizened and dark in the dim light, the white tufts on top barely visible. Their smell was putrid, like rotting garbage swimming in formaldehyde.

Edison walked toward Parrot.

The switchblade was impaled at a forty-five degree angle, inches from Parrot's crotch.

Parrot lay writhing. He looked up at Edison.

"Get it out of me, man..."

Edison put both knees on Parrot's chest and grabbed the switchblade with both hands.

Parrot screamed.

His eyes bulged and his gray lips curled back

as Edison pulled out the switchblade and held it's bloody blade to Parrot's throat.

Taking the tip of the blade away, Edison dragged a peyote button toward Parrot's face. He used the knife to cut the cactus into two parts. He lifted one half on the point of the knife and guided it toward Parrot's open mouth.

"No," Parrot screamed. "That white shit's poison. You can't..."

Edison forced the first cube in Parrot's mouth.

"Eat it, you son-of-a-bitch," Edison said, shifting his weight on Parrot's chest from one knee to the other.

He cut up another of the buttons and then another.

He held the tip of the switchblade against Parrot's lips.

Parrot started to chew.

"That's good," Edison said.

Still holding Parrot, he dumped the bag out. There might have been two dozen shriveled peyote buttons which rolled out onto the floor next to Parrot.

"You're eating all of these," Edison said.

Trinity pulled Lisa to her feet.

Parrot screamed again.

Edison tossed the switchblade to the side and began to pry Parrot's teeth apart with his club.

When it was finished, it would be a flute.

Trinity put his arm around Lisa, turned her face away from Parrot and walked her toward the door.

SOBER

Edward Brooks looked at his daughter.

He stood in a bathrobe in the doorway of his house.

One o'clock in the morning.

He was sober.

"Daddy," she said. "I'm..."

An ugly bruise was forming over her eye.

"God," he said. "Thank God you're safe."

He held her in his arms.

Trinity edged away from the doorway and walked back in the darkness to his Bronco.

GOODBYE, MY BROTHER

Edison looked over the stone wall of the canyon's rest area.

It felt good to leave Tucson behind. He didn't want to think about going back to Holbrook, although he knew eventually he would. He would have to see Tasha and tell her what had happened.

He would even have to see Duane.

Really, he couldn't be too angry at his younger brother who hadn't had any idea what he was setting in motion.

He thought about Pamela and shook his head.

Thank God he hadn't killed her.

It frightened him to think that might have happened.

Eventually he would have to come to terms with that.

In a way, it was like awakening from a dream.

A dream he recalled with vivid detail.

Looking down over the steep canyon walls,

Edison traced the current of the Salt River with an outstretched finger. Clouds drifted below Edison and two crows drifted upwards on a favorable draft of wind.

Livingston's voice was silent now and Edison expected it to stay that way.

He hadn't heard his brother's voice since he left Parrot at the motel.

Edison's mind was silent.

Parrot would live, of course.

He hadn't killed him.

In a way, Edison was glad of that.

A pulse had been beating on Parrot's bluish temple when Edison had shined the flashlight one last time upon Livingston's killer.

But the pulse was all that moved.

Parrot's head lay in a pool of vomit and blood, the mescaline deep inside him. His mouth had been pulled back in a rigid mask, his eyes staring past the light, into the depths of an infinite void.

The spirits in Livingston's visions may have been benign. He had told Edison about some of them.

Then there were the other spirits. The destroying spirits.

Spirits which would make a person wish for the relief of a nightmare.

Edison sensed that Parrot had seen the latter.

He shaded his eyes and looked over the edge of the deep canyon edge to where, far below, rain had replenished the Salt River.

Edison walked around back of the F-150 and hefted the filthy backpack. A few of the buttons remained stuck to the bottom of the pack. Buttons he hadn't been able to bring himself to force down Parrot's throat.

Enough was enough, after all.

Justice had been served.

Edison couldn't hear Livingston's voice anymore, but he remembered his brother's words.

"Show me some respect, Little Brother."

Edison gripped the handle of the bag, feeling the weight. Stooping over, he tossed a couple of stones from the edge of the canyon wall into the sack to increase the weight.

He left the top open.

Lifting the bag over his head, he started to slowly twirl it like a sling. The weight of the stones kept the bag aloft as Edison increased the speed. He felt the bag tugging against his hands, obeying the urge of centrifugal force.

He was reminded of Livingston.

When Edison was only eight years old, Livingston took him out into a pasture and showed him how to rope, slinging the lasso above Edison's head until he finally released it toward the green plastic steer's head, anchored on a hay bale behind the house.

Edison's eyes filled with tears.

Livingston had held Edison's small hand and whispered encouragement at the little boy's effort, whooping with delight when Edison's rope fell over the horns.

When he could not increase it's speed, Edison let go of the backpack and watched it arc into the abyss of the canyon.

"Goodbye, my brother," Edison said softly. "Goodbye, Livingston."

Edison closed his eyes and listened, waiting for the sound of the bag hitting the canyon floor.

He only heard the sound of the river and the wind.

PROSPECTING

Trinity woke up.

How long had he slept? It might have been days. The phone was ringing. It rang three times before he could reach it.

Ray Farmer from the Pinal County Sheriff's Department was on the line.

"Just checking in with you, Trinity. We found that guy you were looking for. Jerome Parroti..."

Trinity nodded.

"I'm happy for you."

"Yeah, Trinity, I'm sure you're pleased. We got an anonymous call late last night. Found the guy overdosed on mescaline in a motel down on Miracle Mile. Big time overdose. Doctors say he might not come back. Mentally, anyway."

"Mescaline, huh?"

Trinity covered the phone and pulled the cord into the kitchen. He thought of the room in the frat set up as a lab, and the overpowering stench created by the mashed buttons.

"That's like peyote, right?"

"You know good and goddamn well what it is,

Trinity. You know anything more about this you haven't told us?"

"Tell you what Ray, give me a few days and then we'll talk."

Farmer wasn't amused.

"Come on, Trinity. This is a courtesy call. The guy had a hole in his leg you could have run a two by four through. Made by his own switchblade, no less. The bastard could have bled to death. I'm trying to be patient, Trinity, but exactly what will we be talking about?"

"Maybe he fell out of bed, Ray. Playing with his knife. I'm going out of town for a while. We'll talk when we get back."

"Look Trinity, don't bother. People OD every day. And you could be right about the switchblade."

"Just trying to be helpful."

"Right Trinity, you're being helpful as hell."

Trinity put the receiver under his arm and grabbed the book he had put on the shelf a few days before.

"I'm going prospecting, Ray. You know any good spots up in Pinal County?"

Farmer had hung up.

Trinity flattened the pages where the water from the cooler had curled them.

Maybe Leslie could take some time off.

Put April in charge of the Presidio Market.

There had to be gold out there somewhere.

ABOUT THE AUTHOR

Trevor Holliday

Trevor Holliday was born in Houston, Texas. While in the Army he served in Turkey and Korea. He taught school in Arizona for over twenty years and in the United Arab Emirates for five. He and his wife Carolyn now live in Fairview Township, Pennsylvania.

BOOKS BY THIS AUTHOR

Trinity Thinks Twice

Trinity And The Short-Timer

Trinity Springs Forward

Trinity And The Heisters

Ferguson's Trip

Dim Lights Thick Smoke

Lefty And The Killers

Trinity Takes Flight

Ten Shots Quick And Other Stories Of The New West

Lefty Brings The Heat

The Forest City

Thanks always to Carolyn Holliday for editing my books and to John Holliday for designing the covers.

Thank *you* for reading Trinity Works Alone.

I hope you will read the rest of the Frank Trinity Novels.
If you enjoyed *Trinity Works Alone*, please consider writing a review on Amazon and telling your friends. As Walter Tevis, writer of *The Hustler* and *The Queen's Gambit* wrote when making the same request: "word of mouth is an author's best friend and much appreciated."

Trevor Holliday